**"What do** [...]
**Natalie** asked softly.

He was quiet for a moment, simply studying her.

"Never mind," she finally said with a weary sigh, not giving him a chance to answer. "I can read it in your face. You expect all women to cut and run, don't you?"

"I guess, Nat, our expectations are based on our past history. And my past history tells me not to expect much from a woman."

"I can understand that. But I think you should understand that I'm unlike any other woman you've ever met, or any nanny you've ever had. I'm me. And I don't cut and run if the going gets tough. Not my style. I have no intention of ever leaving the boys, Jared. Not ever."

\* \* \*

Don't miss next month's installment!
*A Family To Be* (SR #1586)

Dear Reader,

Calling all royal watchers! This month, Silhouette Romance's Carolyn Zane kicks off our exciting new series, ROYALLY WED: THE MISSING HEIR, with the gem *Of Royal Blood*. Fans of last year's ROYALLY WED series will love this thrilling four-book adventure, filled with twists and turns—and of course, plenty of love and romance. Blue bloods and commoners alike will also enjoy Laurey Bright's newest addition to her VIRGIN BRIDES thematic series, *The Heiress Bride*, about a woman who agrees to marry to protect the empire that is rightfully hers.

This month is also filled with earth-shattering secrets! First, award-winning author Sharon De Vita serves up a whopper in her latest SADDLE FALLS title, *Anything for Her Family*. Natalie McMahon is much more than the twin boys' nanny— she's their mother! And in Karen Rose Smith's *A Husband in Her Eyes*, the heroine has her eyesight restored, only to have haunting visions of a man and child. Can she bring love and happiness back into their lives?

Everyone likes surprises, right? Well, in Susan Meier's *Married Right Away*, the heroine certainly gives her boss the shock of his life—she's having his baby! And Love Inspired author Cynthia Rutledge makes her Silhouette Romance debut with her modern-day Cinderella story, *Trish's Not-So-Little Secret*, about "Fatty Patty" who comes back to her hometown a beautiful swan—and a single mom with a jaw-dropping secret!

We hope this month that you feel like a princess and enjoy the royal treats we have for you from Silhouette Romance.

Happy reading!

*Mary-Theresa Hussey*

Mary-Theresa Hussey
Senior Editor

Please address questions and book requests to:
Silhouette Reader Service
U.S.: 3010 Walden Ave., P.O. Box 1325, Buffalo, NY 14269
Canadian: P.O. Box 609, Fort Erie, Ont. L2A 5X3

# Anything for Her Family

## SHARON DE VITA

SILHOUETTE *Romance*®

Published by Silhouette Books

America's Publisher of Contemporary Romance

This one's for my children—all my children.
For Wendy and Glen,
thank you for making me part of the family.
To Rocco, my newest son-in-law, we love you; welcome.
For Jeanne, Annie and Joey, you guys continue to amaze me and make me proud of the people you've become.
I love you all.
Mom

SILHOUETTE BOOKS

ISBN 0-373-19580-X

ANYTHING FOR HER FAMILY

Copyright © 2002 by Sharon De Vita

Visit Silhouette at www.eHarlequin.com

**Printed in U.S.A.**

---

## SHARON DE VITA,

a former adjunct professor of literature and communications, is a *USA Today* bestselling, award-winning author of numerous works of fiction and nonfiction. Her first novel won a national writing competition for Best Unpublished Romance Novel of 1985. This award-winning book, *Heavenly Match,* was subsequently published by Silhouette in 1985. With over two million copies of her novels in print, Sharon's professional credentials have earned her a place in *Who's Who in American Authors, Editors and Poets* as well as in the *International Who's Who of Authors.* In 1987 Sharon was the proud recipient of the *Romantic Times* Lifetime Achievement Award for Excellence in Writing.

A newlywed, Sharon met her husband while doing research for one of her books. The widowed, recently retired military officer was so wonderful, Sharon decided to marry him after she interviewed him! Sharon and her new husband have seven grown children, five grandchildren, and currently reside in Arizona.

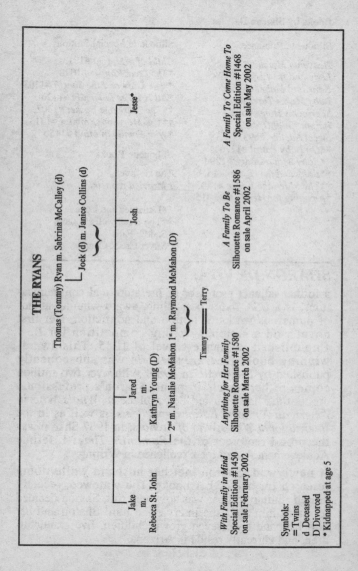

# THE RYANS

Thomas (Tommy) Ryan m. Sabrina McCalley (d)

Jock (d) m. Janice Collins (d)

Jake
m.
Rebecca St. John

Jared
m.
Kathryn Young (D)
2nd m. Natalie McMahon 1st m. Raymond McMahon (D)

Timmy = Terry

Josh

Jesse*

*With Family in Mind*
Special Edition #1450
on sale February 2002

*Anything for Her Family*
Silhouette Romance #1580
on sale March 2002

*A Family To Be*
Silhouette Romance #1586
on sale April 2002

*A Family To Come Home To*
Special Edition #1468
on sale May 2002

Symbols:
= Twins
d Deceased
D Divorced
* Kidnapped at age 5

# *Chapter One*

*Saddle Falls, Nevada*

Natalie McMahon's heart was in her throat as she watched the two little boys with a mangy mutt between them trudging slowly down the hill toward her car.

For a moment, her heart seemed to stop, and she merely stared, unable to believe her eyes.

*Her boys.*

Even after three years, she'd recognize her babies anywhere. There was absolutely no doubt in her mind. *None.*

Her heart recognized the twin babies of her womb with the knowledge only a mother had.

Gasping, she covered her mouth with her hand as tears filled her eyes. The ache that had lived in her heart for the past three years, ever since the day her ex-husband, Raymond, had kidnapped her children, seemed to ease, replaced by the intense joy of overwhelming love.

"My babies." The whisper slipped from her lips as tears spilled. Tears of joy, of disbelief, of love.

Blinking, Natalie feasted her eyes on her babies, going over each one from the top of his glossy black head to the tips of his scruffy sneakers.

The urge to jump from the car, scoop them into her arms and run as fast and as far as possible was nearly overwhelming. But she knew she could never do that.

It was far too dangerous.

Raymond's rein of terror hadn't ended once he'd abducted the boys. No, once the twins were gone, he'd contacted her and told her that if she ever tried to find her children, if she ever made any attempt to locate them, he'd make the twins pay, and pay dearly.

A trickle of fear slid over her, chilling her, but Natalie forced it away, clenching her fists in determination. Never again would she allow Raymond to hurt or terrorize her children.

In spite of the emotions churning through her, and the need to just hold her sons to her aching, lonely heart, Natalie knew she had to remain in firm control of herself *and* her emotions.

It was the only way to protect her sons from their father.

She'd been in Saddle Falls, Nevada, since yesterday. The moment she'd received the call from Harry Powers, the investigator who'd been working her case almost from the moment the boys had disappeared, she'd flown from her home in Chicago to Saddle Falls.

She'd known full well it could be just another wild-goose chase—there'd been many over the past three years—yet she still had to come. Something about *this* time seemed different, perhaps because for the first time everything Harry had discovered added up.

He'd spotted a picture of the boys in an article about the Ryan family in the *Saddle Falls News*. Every year since the boys disappeared, Harry had had their photos digitally age-enhanced so that he'd recognize the boys if he ran across them. Once he saw the recently published picture, he'd traveled to Saddle Falls. His suspicions were confirmed when he checked school records, learned the boys' new names and then went to the county to check their fingerprints on their birth certificates. When a child was adopted, a new birth certificate was issued, but fingerprints never changed.

Perhaps because Harry had been so certain this time, Natalie had decided to come to Saddle Falls, too. She wanted—no, needed—to see for herself if these were truly her babies.

And more importantly, she needed to know everything about Jared Ryan, the man who had adopted her precious sons.

*Adopted.*

Natalie shook her head, still unable to believe that Raymond had stolen her children and then fraudulently put them up for adoption. He'd done it for revenge, to strike back at her because she wouldn't ask her father to drop the criminal charges against him.

Raymond had worked for her father for almost ten years, and all that time he'd apparently been embezzling money from her father's firm. Once her father had discovered the embezzlement, he'd asked Raymond to return the money. When Raymond refused, her father had no choice but to file criminal charges against him.

By that time, Natalie and Raymond's marriage was all but over. Shortly after the twins were born, she'd realized that the man she'd married was both a liar and a cheat, and more importantly, that Raymond was coldly indifferent to the babies she adored.

When she'd finally realized her husband's true nature, she'd filed for divorce. Shortly thereafter, her father had told her about the embezzlement. She'd been both horrified and ashamed, but not really surprised—not by that time.

After the criminal charges were filed, Raymond had been arrested. While out on bond, he'd come to Natalie and tried to intimidate her into having her father drop the charges against him. She'd adamantly refused, even though Raymond had warned that if she didn't, she'd live to regret it.

She'd never expected he would steal the boys to get back at her. But he had, thus beginning a three-year nightmare as she tried to locate her children—a nightmare that had ended with her arrival in Saddle Falls yesterday.

Located about ninety miles from busy, bustling Las Vegas, Saddle Falls was a small, prosperous ranching community populated by second, third and even fourth generations of ranchers. It had pretty scenery, with the top of Mt. Charleston gleaming in the distance. It also had a charming small town feel to it. Not that much different from small towns everywhere.

She'd learned that Tommy Ryan, patriarch of the Ryan clan, had also been one of the founding fathers of Saddle Falls. The Ryan ranch was a sprawling five thousand acre working ranch with a main ranch house fronting the property, and numerous other buildings and bunk houses to house some of the rest of the Ryan family as well as the ranch hands. There was also a large tree house, she'd been told, that had been on the Ryan ranch for two generations now.

Everything she'd learned about the Ryans since she'd arrived in town had both eased her mind and troubled it. They were the most prominent family in the area, well thought of and certainly well respected.

Although horrified at the thought of someone else raising her children, Natalie knew that, if she was ever going to get her children back, if she was ever going to ensure their safety, she would need to know what kind of man Jared Ryan was and if he knew the children he'd adopted had been kidnapped.

Yesterday, she'd also learned that Jared Ryan had been advertising for a nanny for the twins. Natalie had promptly decided on a plan for easing her way back into the boys' life: she would apply for the job.

The irony of applying to become a nanny to her own children was not lost on her. But she wasn't even certain the boys would remember her. They'd been with Jared Ryan longer than they'd been with her, she thought sadly, and because of that, she couldn't simply walk in and claim them, not without frightening them, and shaking their foundation of stability and security.

Becoming a part of their daily life in order to get close to them, and letting them get to know her and feel comfortable with her so she could once again claim them seemed the only solution.

It might not be the *perfect* solution, but for now it was the only option she had available. Becoming the boys' nanny would also help conceal from Jared Ryan who she really was. Until she knew for certain that he had not been connected with Raymond in any way, she felt safer keeping her identity to herself. The boys' safety was her number one priority.

Carefully, Natalie pushed her sunglasses atop her head and took a deep breath, suddenly wondering why the boys were wandering around outside alone.

As if sensing her stress, Ditka, the dog she'd bought the boys for their second birthday and had brought along with her, hoping the boys might remember him, raised his head from the back seat where he'd been sleeping, and turned to stare out the window. The dog gave a plaintive wail, as if he recognized the boys, then went wild, jumping and barking, pawing frantically at the closed window in an effort to get out.

"All right, boy. All right." Natalie reached over and opened the back door before Ditka went right through the window in his excitement. "Go. Go to the boys."

Barking wildly, he bounded around the car toward the twins, who stopped and grinned, pointing and laughing as the large dog raced around them, then rolled on his back like a drunken lunatic.

The mangy mutt with the boys went wild, too, jumping and barking, but one of the twins had a firm grip on his collar, holding on for dear life, lest the dog get loose.

Watching the scene, Natalie felt emotions clog her throat, and she had to swallow hard, forcing herself to behave nonchalantly, as if this was no more important than a lazy afternoon walk.

But her heart knew differently. It felt as if it would burst out of her chest, and she wasn't entirely sure she could control the tears of joy and relief as she slowly slid out of the car and walked toward her long-lost children.

The boys were gone.

Frowning behind his mirrored sunglasses, Jared Ryan tried to bank the panic that clenched his gut as he stood on the long, winding drive of the main ranch house and glanced around, looking for his sons.

He'd been out back, replacing some stones in the patio, while Timmy and Terry played in their playhouse. It was a quick job, something to occupy him, and more importantly, the *boys*, while Mrs. Taylor, their cook and housekeeper, finished dinner.

Mrs. Taylor had been with them forever, but was getting on in years. Although she dearly loved the twins, it was hard to cook with them underfoot, or in Terry's case, continually asking questions. So keeping the boys occupied at dinnertime had become a daily event.

After a day that had started way before sunrise in order to get all the ranch chores done, Jared would have much preferred a cold beer and a soft chair by now. But the twins came first—always.

He'd decided to come around the side of the house to check on the boys simply because they'd been quiet—too quiet. Silence was always dangerous where his sons were concerned.

Good thing he had, he decided with a worried frown, as he started walking down the driveway. The boys knew they weren't allowed off the ranch, at least not without an adult. It was one of Jared's few cardinal rules.

Admittedly, he was perhaps a bit paranoid about the boys' safety and security, but he had good reason to be. Twenty years ago his youngest brother, Jesse, had mysteriously disappeared from this very house. Never to be seen again, Jared recalled with a heavy sigh.

He hated to admit that his brother's disappearance was the first thing that ran through his mind when he came around the front of the house and found the boys gone, or why he felt so panicky.

The memory of what had happened to his little brother had left a deep-seated fear in him that he'd never been able to shake. That fear had merely magnified now that he had children of his own, which was why he was so strict about the boys never being out alone or leaving the ranch.

He'd been very explicit about it—repeatedly. So for the twins to directly disobey him, something they'd never, ever done before... Jared shook his head. Something was up.

Something *big*.

Which was nothing unusual, he thought as he continued

down the driveway, calling their names. Whenever the twins were up to something, it usually meant trouble.

Big trouble.

The kind that could give grown men gray hairs.

In spite of the fact that his beloved boys got into more mischief, more trouble, more misadventures than Jared and his own brothers ever had, his love was total and unconditional.

But he had to admit not everyone appreciated his twins' exuberance for life. Especially the nannies he'd hired, he thought with a wince. Picking up his pace, he searched both sides of the road, sweeping his gaze back and forth in an effort to spot the boys. He'd gone through ten nannies in ten months, which he figured was probably a record somewhere.

It was also why he'd been advertising in the *Saddle Falls News,* without much success, for a new nanny for the past six weeks.

Ever since his wife had left him, barely six months after they'd adopted the twins, he'd been both mother and father to the boys. However, with all his other responsibilities, he worried that the boys were suffering, missing the quality attention they deserved. That they'd miss out on anything was a possibility he couldn't tolerate.

Marrying again was out, not even a consideration, he thought, unaware of how his jaw and fists clenched at the mere thought. He'd learned his lesson the first time when his wife, Kathryn, up and left him and the boys simply because she didn't think she was cut out for motherhood.

Too bad she hadn't figured that out *before* they'd adopted the boys, Jared thought with a scowl. But he was not a man to lament a mistake, and Kathryn had been a big mistake, one he never intended to repeat. Never again would he trust a woman.

When he'd tried to explain to the toddlers that their mother was gone, the look of pain, fear and confusion on their faces had been tattooed on his heart, and he'd vowed to never, ever let another woman close enough to hurt any of them.

So remarriage was out of the question. But a nanny, someone he could *pay* to take care of the boys, and hopefully give them the kind of female attention and affection they desperately needed, without any kind of emotional entanglements or involvement on his part, was a possible alternative.

Unfortunately, finding the right nanny had become another enormous task he had to handle, one he was dutifully working on. But until he found her, he simply focused on being mother and father to the boys, focused on trying to make their lives happy and wonderful.

Just as his had been.

A flicker of fear mixed with hope filled his chest as he heard barking. He frowned for a moment. The boys never went anywhere without their faithful mutt, Ruth, but if he wasn't mistaken, Jared heard two dogs.

With a sigh, he picked up his pace, determined to follow the sound of the barking, certain he'd find his sons.

"Is this your dog?" one of the twins asked Natalie with a laugh, bending to pet Ditka, who leaped up to lick his face, nearly toppling him over.

Seeing the joy on her son's face, Natalie suddenly laughed in turn, her spirits suddenly lighter than they'd been in three years. It was as if a lead weight had been lifted from her heart and she could breathe freely again.

"It is, indeed," she said with another laugh, catching Ditka by the collar and bringing him to heel.

"We like dogs," the other twin said shyly, glancing up at Natalie. "This is our dog, his name is Ruth."

"Ruth?" Still holding on to Ditka, Natalie glanced at the dog, wondering about his name. It was clearly a male. "Your dog's name is Ruth?" she asked with a slight frown.

The first twin grinned, scratching his head. "It's short for Ruthless. He likes us."

"Yes, I can see that," Natalie said with a smile, pretending to focus her attention on the boys' mutt. She wanted to touch her sons so badly! She wanted to press kisses to their faces, to press her cheek to their silky hair, to brush down the cowlicks on their heads.

She wanted to do everything she'd been denied for so many years. The urge was strong, a yearning that made her hands itch and her arms ache, so she tucked her free hand in the pocket of her yellow jean shorts, and clutched Ditka's collar tighter with the other. She had to remember she was supposedly a stranger to the boys. They apparently didn't recognize her. If they had, they would have obviously said something by now. Natalie didn't want to do anything to frighten them.

"Well, Ditka likes little boys, too." She glanced down affectionately at the dog, who'd laid his head on one of the twins' shoes, and was staring adoringly up with large eyes. "Don't you, boy?" Ditka gave a confirming bark, making Ruth answer in kind, and the boys giggled again.

"My name's Terry," the one in the green shirt said with a grin. "This is Timmy." Terry elbowed his brother—who wore a blue shirt—in the ribs. "We're twins."

Natalie gave a sigh of relief that the boys' first names had not been changed. "Twins?" She leaned down, pretending to peer at their faces. "Mmm, yes, I can see a resemblance," she said with a grin.

"I'm older," Timmy said, elbowing his brother back.

"Yeah, but I'm smarter," Terry countered with a giggle, revealing the family trait of dimples. He tilted his chin toward her. "What's your name?"

"Natalie," she said softly, watching her sons' face for any sign of recognition. There was none, and she tried not to let it hurt. "Uh...where are you boys going? Are you supposed to be out by yourselves?"

The twins exchanged guilty looks. "It's not dark yet," Terry said evasively, making Natalie frown.

"No," she said carefully, realizing there was probably more to this story than they were letting on. "It's not."

"Dad says we can't be out after dark." Timmy scratched his head. "It's not dark yet," he repeated, as if confirming the fact again. "And we're not alone." He tightened his hold on Ruth. "We have Ruth with us."

"Yes, I can see that," Natalie said. "But where are you going?"

"We're running away," Terry offered with a wide, guileless grin, making Timmy groan and roll his eyes.

Horrified, Natalie tried not to panic. She looked from one child to the other again. They looked perfectly healthy and in good shape, but perhaps looks were deceiving. Perhaps she'd been misled about the Ryans.

"Running away?" Her glance went from one to the other again. "But why are you running away?"

"Cuz of a stupid, smelly girl," Timmy offered miserably.

"Lucy the frog-face," Terry added just as glumly.

"A girl?" Natalie relaxed a fraction and tried to contain a smile. "I see." She nodded. "And what did this, uh, girl do?" she asked with a deliberately serious expression.

"She kissed Timmy," Terry said, unable to stop a giggle. "Lucy kissed him smack on the cheek." The fit of giggles blossomed until Timmy gave him a whack. "On the playground right in front of everyone."

"It's not funny," Timmy argued, whacking his brother again. "And it's not your tongue Lucy's brother's gonna rip out and paint the school building with."

"I imagine it must be pretty scary, having a girl kiss you in front of all your friends." Deliberately, Natalie tucked her tongue in her cheek to stop another smile.

"Uh-huh." Timmy rolled of his eyes. "That's why we're running away." He sighed. "When Lucy kissed me I…I called her frog-face and she started to cry, and so her brother—"

"Threatened to rip your tongue out," Natalie finished with a knowing nod, trying to hide her amusement. "I think I understand. So you're running away so you don't have to go to school and face Lucy's brother, is that it?"

The boys exchanged wide-eyed glances, wondering how she'd guessed. Timmy shrugged. "Yeah, I guess so."

"Ahh," Natalie said with a nod. "But did you tell your mom where you were going? Just so she won't worry when she realizes you're gone?" She almost choked on the words.

Timmy sobered immediately and the boys exchanged sad looks. "Uh…we don't got a mother," he stated, scuffing the toe of his sneaker in the dirt. "She went away a long time ago."

"But we got a father," Terry countered with a crooked grin. "A real cool father. His name's Jared. And we got two uncles and a grandpop." He turned and pointed. "We live right over there, the big ranch just over the hill."

She nodded. "Well, does your father know you're, uh, running away?" Her gaze shifted from one face to the other as they exchanged sheepish glances. "Thought so," she said with a nod. She took a deep breath, trying to think how to handle this. "I'm sure your dad's going to be very scared when he finds out you're gone. Don't you think you should let him know you're running away? I mean, just so he won't worry about what happened to you?"

Timmy scuffed the toe of his sneaker in the dust again. "We…we, uh, didn't think about Dad being scared," he said, casting a guilty look at his brother. "Did we?"

"Nope. We didn't." Terry's eyes widened and he blinked up at Natalie. "Do dads get scared?" he asked her with a slight frown. He shoved a strand of hair off his forehead. "I thought only kids got scared."

Natalie wanted to laugh. Her sons may have grown and changed, but their personalities, which she had only caught a hint when they were age two, had blossomed. Terry was just as curious and inquisitive as he had been as a toddler. Somehow she found that reassuring, as if the time and distance that had separated them was not that wide.

"Oh, yes, definitely," she said with a nod. "Moms and dads get just as scared as kids, and I'll bet when your dad finds out you're gone, he's going to be very scared."

"Uh-oh." Timmy poked his brother with his elbow. "There's Dad now." The little boy swallowed hard. "And he doesn't look scared, Terry. He looks mad."

"Double uh-oh," Terry said glumly, glancing past his brother to see his dad barreling toward them, his long legs eating up the distance at a pace that would scare anyone. "Timmy," he groaned. "I think we're in trouble. Big trouble," he whispered, then sighed. *"Again."*

Natalie glanced up and her breath nearly withered at the sight of the large man coming toward them. He didn't seem the friendly type.

Furious, definitely. Not friendly.

She couldn't stop the shiver that rolled over her, chilling her at her first sight of Jared Ryan.

His legs were long, muscled, and ate up the ground like a hungry panther, making her feel like prey.

The sight of him caused Ditka to start barking and jumping again, straining against his collar. Ruth followed suit, creating a cacophony.

"Ditka. Stay," Natalie ordered, giving the dog's collar a gentle tug. But he tugged right back, nearly knocking her off balance in her high-heeled sandals. "Ditka!" He broke loose and Ruth followed, nearly knocking Timmy over before the two dogs bounded, barking and yipping, toward Jared Ryan.

Feeling helpless, Natalie watched as the large man reached down with one fluid motion and corralled both dogs by their collars. He continued toward her and the twins, tugging the dogs along with him, his dark, intense gaze never leaving Natalie's.

"Lady!" His deep voice boomed, nearly vibrating the ground beneath her feet. "What the hell do you think you're doing with my children?"

"Wait, Dad," Timmy said, stepping between his father and her. "This is Natalie. She's our friend. She wasn't doing nothing but talking to us, honest."

Jared barely gave Natalie a glance as she reached for Ditka's leash. Hearing his son's voice, seeing that both boys were safe, immediately quelled the panic inside of him, but the edginess of fear remained.

Determined to get himself under control, he glanced down at the twins, realizing he'd probably frightened them. A wave of regret washed over him. He'd never raised his voice in front of the boys before, but he'd been so frightened to find them gone that his own fears had overruled his common sense for a moment.

Jared bent down so he was eye level with his sons, wrapping his long arms around them and drawing them close, needing to touch them, to verify they were safe.

"Your friend, huh?" he repeatedly suspiciously. He deliberately softened his tone, then ruffled Timmy's hair, smiling at Terry. "So you guys want to tell me why you left the ranch when you know it's against the rules?" He didn't give the boys a chance to answer, but spared Natalie another searing glance. "And why you're talking to a stranger when you know that's against the rules, as well?"

"But Dad," Terry protested. "We told you, she's our friend."

"Mr. Ryan? My name is Natalie McMahon and perhaps I can explain."

Jared had no idea who this woman was or why she thought she was capable of explaining to him what *his* sons were doing. Fierce paternal protectiveness reared up inside of him, along with a huge wave of annoyance.

"Fine." He almost snapped the word. Still keeping the twins close, Jared stood. "Why don't you start by explaining to me who you are and what you're doing with my boys?" His voice was still harsher than he intended, but it couldn't be helped. He didn't like strangers anywhere near his sons.

"I'm here to interview for the nanny position," she said simply, stunning Jared. "I, uh, phoned earlier today and was told by someone that I should come by about this time to see you."

"*Nanny?*" Jared slowly removed his sunglasses and took a good look at her. His jaw almost hit the ground and his suspicions rose again. If this was a nanny, he was the king of Siam.

She was, in a word, gorgeous. A bit too thin and fragile for his tastes, but a looker nonetheless, with long, tanned legs that seemed to go on forever in spite of her size, which was slender and petite. Perhaps it was the high-heeled sandals or the thigh-high, sunny yellow shorts that made her legs seem so long.

The T-shirt she wore, in a shade of yellow that made the sun seem pale in comparison, matched her jean shorts and fit nicely over very lush, lovely feminine curves, the kind that made a man's mouth go dry.

Sunglasses shielded her eyes from the sun, while a curtain of jet-black hair tumbled to her shoulders, swaying gently in the light afternoon breeze, giving his heart a familiar bump. A bump that annoyed him because it reminded him that he was still alive, still a virile man with normal, healthy appetites.

Well, he thought with a scowl, letting his gaze run leisurely over the petite woman again, he might still have normal, healthy appetites, but that didn't mean he ever intended to get tangled up with another woman and let her make a fool out of him. Or worse, hurt the boys.

But it also didn't mean he couldn't appreciate the pleasurable sight of a beautiful woman, he decided, letting his gaze roam over her again. Looking was fine. It was all he'd allowed himself in the past three years.

It was all the other stuff that went into male-female relationships that could get a guy into trouble.

"So…Natalie, is it?" he asked with a lift of his brow.

"Yes," she said quietly. "I'm Natalie McMahon."

"Well, Ms. McMahon, why don't we go into the house and discuss this?" He wanted a chance to find out who this woman really was and what she really wanted—without the boys around. "Shall we?" Jared didn't give her a chance to respond, he simply hustled the boys and Ruth up the road, leaving Natalie and Ditka staring after them, with little choice but to follow.

# *Chapter Two*

She was never going to get hired now, Natalie thought in a panic, swallowing back tears of frustration as she paced the length of Jared Ryan's study.

Outside, it had been clear to her that the man was suspicious. There was little she could do about it, so she'd gotten in her car and followed him to his house, hoping to settle her fears. The thought of not doing what he'd asked—what he'd *ordered,* she amended in annoyance—simply never occurred to her. She'd really had no choice. She'd come too far to turn away now, not without her children.

As soon as she'd parked in the long, winding driveway, Jared had escorted her from the car and into the house, without giving her a chance to say a word.

He'd led her to his study and told her to wait for him, that he'd be back in a minute as soon as he got the boys settled in their rooms. He'd shut the door firmly behind him, leaving her annoyed and staring after him, wondering if he was always so bossy.

Natalie shook her head, trying to calm her jagged nerves.

Waiting for Jared Ryan to return, she felt like a prisoner waiting for the executioner.

And she didn't much like the feeling.

As Natalie paced, she glanced around the spacious room. It was cluttered but clean, filled with large, masculine pieces of furniture. She hadn't had much of a chance to see any more of the house, but this was clearly a working office.

There was a large oak desk in the middle of the room, scarred a bit from age and use, but everything on it— several stacks of papers, seed and feed catalogs, bills of lading, and an assortment of other paraphernalia—was neatly arranged. The old, black, rotary dial phone nestled in the corner made her smile. Obviously Jared must be sentimental about some things.

Large, nearly floor to ceiling windows filled the wall opposite the desk, left bare to allow the hazy golden light of early evening to spill in, casting the room in a soft glow.

The other three spacious walls were lined with bookcases filled with an interesting assortment of books, she noted: biographies, history, classics, even some current bestsellers. Two shelves held volumes on ranching and raising cattle. There were also books on strange cattle diseases, and for good measure, a well-worn copy of a baby and child care book, with several pages dog-eared and turned down. It made her smile, because she had one just like it at home, from when the twins were born. It had been her Bible when she was a new mother with two colicky babies.

On the credenza behind the desk sat a very modern computer with a small, efficient-looking printer lined up neatly next to it.

Nearby was an assortment of framed pictures of the twins at various ages. They instantly drew Natalie's attention, and she stood there, soaking in the sight of her children as they'd grown and changed. Each picture had a small caption underneath identifying their age when the picture had been taken.

In each photo, the boys wore matching, lopsided grins, and identical clothes, except for their T-shirts, which were different colors—probably so Jared could identify who was who.

Tears filled her eyes as she reverently touched each photograph, memorizing the changes that were graphically revealed.

Looking at the pictures reminded her of all she had missed in her children's lives, all she'd been robbed of because of the cruel selfishness of her ex-husband.

And made her all the more determined to do whatever was necessary to claim her precious sons once again.

Natalie's fists clenched in determination and her eyes squeezed shut as a bout of pure panic rose. What she was doing terrified her because she was so fearful that Raymond might somehow learn she'd found the boys. The last thing she wanted was to put her children in jeopardy once again! But she wasn't about to turn tail and bolt. Not now, not ever. Not until the boys were safely in her care again.

"Ms. McMahon?" Jared Ryan's deep, resonant voice startled her, and Natalie whirled to find him leaning against the doorjamb, his gaze leisurely taking her in.

Not quite certain if she liked being measured by him, she forced herself to boldly meet his gaze, even though it made her quiver inside like a sapling in a storm.

Looking into his eyes, she found her mouth going dry, and she swallowed hard. The way he was looking at her, with such quiet intensity, made her pulse leap and her heart somersault.

Jared Ryan was definitely *not* what she'd expected, she

realized dully. He was, she decided, the kind of man any woman would notice.

He was much bigger than she'd envisioned, at least six four or five, with a well-toned, muscular body that projected an intense masculinity. Well-worn jeans, thin at the knees, frayed at the cuffs, fit his muscled legs like a glove. The hand-tooled but scruffy boots he wore added even more height to the big man.

The plaid, chambray work shirt he wore was nearly threadbare in spots and stretched across wide shoulders obviously broadened by heavy work.

There was a dark intensity about him and his gaze that reminded her of cowboys of the Wild West.

His hair was inky black, and worn long enough to graze the collar of his work shirt. His eyes were an incredible shade of blue—almost silver, like a wolf. He had a sculptured mouth that fit his face perfectly.

His features were harsh, blunt, and yet beautiful in a stark, masculine way. Confidence radiated from him in waves, enough to make any woman immediately take note.

With his gaze still measuring her, Natalie found she had to swallow again, wishing she wasn't quite so aware of him. It was unnerving.

"Please have a seat." His words sounded more like another order than a polite request, but though his tone of voice made her bristle, she did as he asked.

When he entered the room to walk around his desk and take his own seat, it seemed as if the space shrunk, bringing her in even closer proximity to him. As he passed, she caught a hint of a masculine scent—no hint of flowery aftershave, but a fragrance so pleasant it almost made her head swim.

Confused by the sudden feelings that Jared Ryan had brought out, Natalie tried to remain calm. She hadn't had much experience with men—certainly not before Raymond, whom she'd met through her father her last year in college, and definitely not after.

Raymond had been the only serious boyfriend she'd ever had. He'd been one of her father's key employees, and she'd felt honored that he'd even noticed her. She'd been very shy and a bit insecure, and found that Raymond's charm had eased the way for her.

Only later did she realize that Raymond's charm was about as lethal as a snakebite, and hid a poisonous nature and intent. Even then Raymond had been embezzling money, and he'd married her simply as insurance. He'd been certain that, if he ever got caught, his wife wouldn't allow him to go to jail. In the end, he'd been just as wrong about her as she'd been about him.

During the three years since she'd divorced him and lost her children, Natalie had concentrated all her energy on finding the twins. The thought of dating was not something she'd even contemplated, let alone considered.

She wasn't certain she could ever trust another man after her experiences. She wasn't the type to condemn a whole gender because of one person, but neither did she trust her own judgment about men. She'd made a terrible mistake with Raymond, a mistake that had destroyed her father and cost her her children. Raymond's embezzlement from her father's firm had bankrupted her dad. And when he'd kidnapped her sons, it had broken her father's heart. Raymond's actions had ruined her and her children's lives.

It was a mistake that had carried a very heavy price and a heavy load of guilt—guilt she was still struggling with on a daily basis.

So being faced with someone as strongly masculine, as well as attractive and confident as Jared Ryan was enough to make her nerves thrum from worry.

Struggling to remain calm, Natalie realized she couldn't do anything to further arouse his suspicions. She had to appear cool, calm and totally collected. As if she had nothing more on her mind than interviewing for this position.

Hiding her simmering emotions and fears was mandatory.

Aware that he was scrutinizing her, Natalie laced her ringless fingers together to stop them from shaking, praying her voice would be calmer than her nerves, and casually crossed one leg over the other, aware that his gaze momentarily followed the movement of her legs.

Finally, he brought his intense gaze to hers. "Ms. Mc-Mahon, I want to apologize for my behavior outside."

"Excuse me?" His apology caught her completely off guard. She'd been fully prepared to go into a lengthy apology and explanation about what *she'd* been doing there, with *his* boys, since he hadn't given her time to thoroughly explain outside. So his comment threw her off balance for a moment.

Not liking the way her stomach seemed to quiver every time she looked into his eyes, Natalie glanced away. Something about the way he focused his gaze on her made her pulse thud inexplicably, made her incredibly aware of her own femininity.

"I said I want to apologize for my behavior outside." He flashed that slow, lazy smile, and Natalie's mind went blank. His smile was megabright and softened the harsh planes of his face. "Mrs. Taylor, our cook, is getting on in years and is a bit forgetful at times, I'm afraid. She just told me that you had called earlier today inquiring about the nanny position."

"Yes, that's true," Natalie replied with a slight frown. "But I told you that outside." Her voice held a hint of accusation, and she made a deliberate effort to soften her stance.

"Yes, I know," he admitted sheepishly.

"But you didn't believe me?"

"I'm sorry..." His voice trailed off and he lifted his hands in supplication. "You see, I'd been working out in the back acres most of the day, at least until the boys came home from school, and Mrs. Taylor neglected to mention to me that you were coming by for an interview." He smiled that lazy smile again and Natalie found herself unable to draw her gaze from it.

She licked her dry lips, realizing that fooling Jared Ryan was not going to be easy. "I told you that outside but—"

"But I wasn't listening." Jared nodded. "I know. Stubbornness is a Ryan trait, I'm afraid." He flashed a grin that made her stomach muscles tighten. "Again, I'm sorry. I didn't mean to be rude, or to scare you, but when it comes to my boys I am admittedly a bit overprotective. We don't get many strangers around here, so when I saw you talking to my sons, I guess I just panicked."

"I understand." It was going to be hard not to bristle every time he called them *his* boys, Natalie realized. The urge to shout that they were *hers* was nearly overwhelming.

"I have very few rules, Ms. McMahon—"

"Natalie, please?" she said with a small smile.

"What?" He blinked at her. He'd been studying her face, those exquisite features, and had missed what she'd said.

"Please call me Natalie."

Jared looked at her, stunned anew by the impact she was having on him. He'd been totally taken aback when Mrs. Taylor had told him Natalie McMahon had indeed called earlier in the day inquiring about the nanny position. The confirmation only added to his embarrassment over his knee-jerk behavior outside.

He let his gaze rake over Natalie again, from the top of her shiny black hair to the tips of her polished toes, bare in her high-heeled sandals. The woman definitely had the kind of legs that could make a man trip over his drooling tongue.

He realized with a frown that she certainly didn't look like any nanny he'd ever seen before.

And the idea of calling her by her first name, inviting that kind of familiarity between them, made him suddenly wary. But then again, he'd been wary around woman for so long it had become habit, he realized. Especially beautiful woman.

He'd deliberately kept his distance from women, all women, not wanting to even consider the possibility of any kind of entanglement. It wouldn't be fair, not when he wasn't prepared to allow a woman into his life—at least not that part of his life that contained his sons. And his sons were his life. So there was really no point.

But now, through no fault of his own, he was face-to-face with a beautiful woman, and Jared found his imagination going haywire. Natalie McMahon was definitely a distraction in his normal humdrum existence.

It made him nervous.

He didn't want a nanny who made him think about the things he'd been missing. He didn't want a woman in his life who heated his blood or stirred his imagination.

However, always practical, Jared realized that the fact that he found her stunningly attractive was *not* a good enough reason to dismiss her without even giving her the courtesy of an interview. She could be perfectly qualified and a jewel of a nanny. He'd never know unless he gave her the benefit of the doubt and talked with her.

Out of fairness, and his own desperation, he owed her that much.

But he would have felt better if she'd been eighty and toothless, Jared thought grimly. He was only human and, he had to admit, a bit lonely. Starved for female companionship, his brother Jake was always telling him.

But he had priorities, he reminded himself firmly, and a woman certainly wasn't one of them. The boys, the ranch and his family—those were his priorities, in that order. He didn't have time for anything or anyone else, especially a woman who was far too beautiful for his peace of mind.

But at this point, especially after what happened today with the boys, he realized he couldn't afford to be picky, nor could he afford to pass up a competent nanny simply because she was a bit too attractive for his liking.

He needed someone to mind the boys so he could work the ranch and handle the rest of his responsibilities without feeling he was neglecting his sons. What happened with the boys today—the two of them wandering off—had scared Jared enough to realize that something had to change—immediately.

He wasn't looking for a wife, he was looking for an employee, and with any luck at all, Natalie McMahon just might fill the bill. He would simply ignore the feelings she aroused in him. He'd learned the hard way that life would be simpler that way, and far, far safer.

"Natalie," he acknowledged with a curt nod, determined to keep some distance between them simply because of the reaction he was having to her. "I don't have a lot of rules, but one of my golden rules is the boys are never allowed off the ranch without an adult with them, nor are they allowed to talk to strangers. Ever." He hesitated. "Since their mother left when they were barely two and a half, I've been both mother and father to them, and their safety and security are of the utmost importance to me.''

"Of course," Natalie said, understanding perfectly. If she'd been more scrupulous about the boys' security, she wouldn't be in the position she was now. But she'd had no idea how desperate, how delusional Raymond had become. She'd never dreamed he would use the boys to get back at her. It was a mistake she'd never ever make again.

"When I came around front to see what the twins were up to and found they were gone…" His voice trailed off and he shook his dark head, paling slightly at the thought. "I panicked," he stated with a shrug. "I'll be the first to admit the boys have given me some wild scares with their antics, but this one…" Blowing out a breath, Jared rubbed a hand over his stubbled jaw, still shaken. "The thought of the boys being gone utterly terrified me." For the second time that day, his mind went back to his little brother Jesse, and he couldn't shake away the thought or the sudden fear.

"The boys know better." A muscle in his jaw twitched when he thought of what could have happened had he not gone to check on them when he had. "So I just don't understand what they were doing, or why they'd directly disobey me. It's not like them." Shaking his head again, Jared leaned back further in his chair and rocked a bit, lost in thought. "Where on earth did they think they were going and why?" he said almost to himself. "Why would they deliberately disobey me?"

"Did you ask them?" Natalie inquired quietly, and Jared looked at her in surprise for a long moment, feeling a bit stung, wondering if she was criticizing his parental abilities.

"No, I guess not." He shook his head, not certain why it was important she understand. "I was too relieved that they were safe, I guess, and too upset that they'd directly disobeyed me. It never occurred to me to ask them *why* they'd disobeyed me.''

Natalie smiled at him, simply because he looked so utterly miserable. ''Being a parent is never easy, and being a single parent is sort of like walking a tightrope backward, wearing high heels that are too big for you.'' She broke off when he laughed at the visual image. ''But we do the best we can and hope it's enough. Sometimes we make mistakes.'' She shrugged. ''Parents aren't perfect, but most mistakes are made out of fear and love—a very weighty, emotional combination for any parent.''

Cocking his head, Jared looked at her with a new appreciation. ''Sounds like you've had a little bit of experience with children?'' The fact that she'd hit the nail on the head with what had happened to him today impressed the hell out of him.

''A little,'' she admitted, shifting uncomfortably. At all costs she wanted to avoid any discussion of her private life. She was not accustomed to lying, and knew that it would be difficult for her to do so now or to make up a believable story.

She'd decided even before coming here that she would tell him as much of the truth as possible, at least a version of the truth that would protect her true identity and why she was really there. It would be far simpler that way. She didn't particularly like the idea of deceiving him. It felt wrong somehow.

''I think you might feel better if you knew the boys weren't deliberately trying to disobey you. They were running away,'' she stated calmly.

''Running away? What on earth makes you say that?''

''I asked,'' she said quietly, shrugging slightly. ''I don't think they even considered the fact that they were disobeying you, at least not consciously. They were just focused on handling their own problem—''

''What problem?'' Jared demanded, wondering what the hell was going on, and more importantly, how he could not be aware of it. ''What kind of problem can two five-year-olds have that would make them run away?'' The thought of anything bothering his boys troubled him. ''And why didn't they come and talk to me about it? They know they can talk to me about anything.''

''I honestly don't know. *That* I didn't have time to ask.''

Wearily, Jared dragged a hand through his hair. ''Whatever it was must have been pretty serious for them to think they had to run away,'' he said, fighting back a bout of fear at the mere thought.

''Well, I'm sure *they* thought it was pretty serious.'' She paused for a moment and her mouth quirked with humor. ''It involved a girl.''

''A girl?'' Jared repeated, still clearly confused. ''But they're five-year-olds,'' he protested, making her laugh.

''Yes, but if you have any experience with male-female relations, I'm sure you know it's never too early to get into trouble with the opposite sex.''

He laughed in turn, and some of the tension left him. ''Well, you're right about that.'' Jared shook his head. ''Okay, so who's the girl and what did the boys do?'' He almost added ''this time,'' but thought it better not to scare her off—just yet.

''Well, I believe the girl is Lucy the frog-face.''

One of his brows rose and Jared eyed Natalie curiously, amusement suddenly glinting in his blue eyes. ''Lucy? The frog-face?'' he repeated, causing her to laugh.

The soft, feminine sound raked along Jared's nerve endings, reminding him how long it had been since he'd been in the company of a beautiful woman.

Too long, he decided. Much too long. But that didn't mean he was going to allow himself any interest in *this* one.

Right now, she was the first decent nanny prospect he'd seen in a long time. She had a sense of humor, an understanding of children and obvious experience with them. He couldn't afford to scare her off.

"Well," Natalie said, "I'm sure that's not the name her mother gave her, but it is the name the boys did."

"I see," he said with a knowing nod. "And let me guess—Lucy took great umbrage at this new name the boys gave her?" he asked with a grin, lifting a finger to rub his brow as understanding dawned.

"Well, her older brother was the one who apparently took great umbrage at her new name." Her smile widened. "Lucy apparently kissed Timmy on the playground in front of everyone. And he in turn—"

"Called her a frog-face?" Jared finished with a nod of understanding. "So Lucy's brother threatened to…what? Rip Timmy's eyes out with fishhooks?"

"Close," she admitted with a smile. "Which means you must have some experience at this?"

Jared laughed. "Lots. Must run in the family. Me and my brothers have been getting into trouble with women since we were old enough to walk."

"I'm not certain I find that very comforting," she said with a laugh, making light of something that made her more than nervous. If Jared Ryan's brothers looked anything like him, she had a feeling they had given mothers and brothers everywhere fits.

Amusement glinted in his eyes and he grinned. "Jake's the oldest, then me, then Josh. We were affectionately known as the town terrors," he said, making her laugh again. "Much to my grandfather Tommy's chagrin."

"Then it should probably not come as any surprise that Lucy's brother apparently threatened to rip out Timmy's tongue and paint the school building with it."

"Ouch." Jared shuddered, then nodded in sudden understanding. "So that's why the boys were running away?"

"You got it."

"Okay, I get the picture. So if I'm following the little munchkins' minds, they were running away so they wouldn't have to go to school tomorrow and face Lucy's brother, right?"

Natalie laughed, surprised by how in tune he was to the boys, and not certain if it was comforting or alarming. "Right." She sighed softly. "I was just trying to convince them to go back home and tell you what they were up to when you arrived."

Cocking his head, he was thoughtful for a moment. "You know, Natalie, it seems to me I should have been thanking you instead of barking at you." He shrugged, feeling a growing sense of comfort with her, something that was very unusual for him. His wariness with women was almost legendary. "I am sorry, but when it comes to the boys, I feel you can never be too careful." He rubbed his stubbled jaw again, wishing he'd had time to shave before interviewing her. "Those boys mean the world to me."

His gaze met hers and Natalie felt a shiver race over her.

*And they meant the world to her, too. But her world had collapsed when they'd been stolen from her.*

She studied Jared, noting the sincerity in his features, the love glinting in his eyes, and she had no doubt, absolutely none, that Jared Ryan loved the boys. She could see it in his face and hear it in his voice.

But they were *her* boys.

Hers.

Banking the twinge of maternal jealousy that had flared

up, she glanced at Jared, and the jealousy was quickly swept away by guilt. She was going to hurt him and she knew it. But there was nothing she could do to prevent it. What was sad was that he was apparently an innocent by-stander in the boys' kidnapping.

He appeared totally innocent.

And she was going to devastate him.

Deliberately and intentionally.

Just as she had been deliberately and intentionally dev-astated. The difference was the act against her had been relished, savored, done deliberately for that purpose.

She, on the other hand, had no choice in the matter.

Cruelty wasn't in her nature. She'd never deliberately hurt anyone in her life, but she was going to have to do so now, for the boys' sake and safety.

She wanted to weep. Weep because Jared Ryan appeared to be a very nice man who was totally devoted to her boys. He'd given them a home, love, a family, and he didn't deserve to have his heart ripped out any more than she had deserved it.

But she didn't have a choice in the matter. The boys were *hers*, legally, morally and in every other way. The fact that Jared Ryan had unwittingly and innocently been included in Raymond's madness made her unbearably sad, but didn't alter the fact that she wanted her children back.

She'd searched so long and so hard to find her children, had missed so much of their lives, that now that she'd found them, she wanted nothing more than to claim them and spirit them away.

But she knew no matter how strong the urge to do just that, she couldn't. She had to be careful and very, very patient. For now, she had to keep up this charade.

She *had* to deliberately deceive Jared Ryan into believing she was just a nanny, because she couldn't and wouldn't take a chance—not even the slightest chance—that Raymond might find out she'd finally found the boys.

She had no idea where her ex-husband was, nor did the authorities, who'd been looking for him since he'd snatched the boys. There was a long list of charges against him stemming from his embezzlement. Since he'd snatched the boys and disappeared while out on bond on the embezzlement charge, additional charges had been filed against him, including kidnapping and flight to avoid prosecution.

But Raymond was far too smart and cunning to allow himself to be caught. Along with that cunning went a brutal cruelty that terrified her.

He'd warned her that he would be keeping an eye on her, warned her that if she tried to find him or the boys, he'd make the boys pay dearly for it. She had no doubt he meant it.

She would never put her boys at risk again—never.

Natalie glanced at Jared, felt the bitter taste of guilt on her tongue, then quickly swallowed it. If keeping her boys safe meant she had to deceive Jared Ryan, so be it.

Her thoughts were interrupted when Jared asked, "So, Natalie, tell me, if I haven't scared you away, do you still want to apply for the position of nanny for my boys?"

"Absolutely." She gave her head a confident toss. "It will take more than a few gruff words to scare me away," she said with a determined lift of her chin.

"Good. Good." Jared leaned back in his chair again, then smiled that slow smile that caused her pulse to thud nervously. "So tell me, why on earth do you want to be a nanny to two very active, rambunctious little boys?"

"I love children," she admitted with a self-conscious smile, not wanting to tell him that she'd always wanted a houseful.

"I know the feeling," Jared said with a nod. "I love

children as well.'' His face grew somber for a moment and he glanced away. ''Unfortunately, my wife was unable to have any.''

''I'm so sorry.'' It was hard not to feel sympathy for him, considering the circumstances.

''No, don't be,'' he said, good humor restored. ''I firmly believe in fate, and adopting the twins turned out to be the best thing that could have happened to me. And them, too, I hope.''

''The twins are adopted?'' she asked, feigning ignorance. This was dangerous ground. It was important to know if Jared Ryan had any connection to Raymond, or any clue about the true background or identity of the boys. Yet she couldn't appear too anxious or too inquisitive about his life.

Even though Harry Powers, the investigator, had assured her he hadn't, she needed to verify it for her own peace of mind, although she doubted that anyone of Jared's caliber would have anything to do with someone like Raymond.

Jared Ryan didn't look like the kind of man to be hood-winked by a smooth talking charmer.

As she had been.

It would do well for her to remember that, she thought.

''Yes, we adopted the twins when they were about two, through a private attorney, but I couldn't love those boys more if they'd been born to me.''

*But they weren't.*

''Do you have any children, Natalie?'' He didn't want to pry, but he needed to know everything about a woman who might be taking care of the most precious beings in his life, especially since she would have such a profound impact on the boys on a day to day basis. ''A family of your own?''

''Children?'' she repeated weakly, feeling as if the floor had dropped out from beneath her. For a moment, everything inside her stilled. Avoiding Jared's penetrating gaze, Natalie glanced down, lacing and unlacing her fingers. "I had two children," she said quietly, unable to look at him. "I...I lost them." The tone of her voice was heartbreakingly sad and clearly did not invite any further question or discussion.

Her words hung in the air for a moment, as if reverberating around and around the room, gathering power. Jared merely stared at her, stunned and at a loss as to what to say.

He knew from experience how empty, how futile words of sorrow and sympathy were when you'd suffered a tremendous personal loss.

"I'm so sorry, Natalie," he said quietly, glancing away, thinking about his own sorrow, his own loss—his brother Jesse.

Even after all these years it was hard to believe the pain was still so raw, so deep.

Yes, he knew full well the unending sorrow she felt, and he wouldn't pry. Not about this.

"But I do have a lot of experience with children," Natalie added, hoping her voice wasn't shaking. She wanted to change the subject. Taking a deep breath, she was grateful it slid out easily and effortlessly. Only then did she dare to glance at Jared, to see that his features had softened, his eyes had filled with compassion.

She refused to acknowledge it, even privately. She couldn't; she had to remain detached and totally unemotional around Jared Ryan. She couldn't afford to care about him or his feelings—no matter how difficult it was. Detached and totally unemotional was the name of the game. If she didn't remain so, it could jeopardize everything she'd worked toward the past three years.

"Mr. Ryan—"

"Jared," he corrected.

"Jared," she repeated quietly. "In addition to my own children, it seems as if I've taken care of someone else's children for as long as I can remember. I was a nanny all through college." Reaching down, she pulled her folded up résumé out of her purse and slid it across the desk to him. "Obviously it's been a few years since college, but there's a list of my employers, and you'll see I worked for one family for just over four years during school."

"I've no doubt you have experience," he said gently, realizing she was every bit as anxious and nervous as he. Somehow he found it charming. "That was clear from the way you handled the boys today." He smiled. "They don't usually talk to strangers, especially female strangers. Since their mother left…" His voice trailed off and he glanced over her head out the windows, as if seeing something visible only to him. "The boys have had a difficult time getting close to females, not that we have an abundance of females in the Ryan family," he added with a grin. "It's just men except for my brother Jake's wife, Rebecca. But clearly the boys liked you." He couldn't help but be pleased at the thought. Having the boys like and accept her would go a long way toward ensuring their happiness.

Her heart warmed and she couldn't help the smile of pleasure that curved her lips. "And I liked them." Eyes dancing, she leaned forward. "They're wonderful boys. Truly. Bright, adventuresome, intelligent."

Paternal pride lit Jared's face. "I like to think so, but I have to warn you, Natalie, you left out something."

"What?"

"They're also a handful," he added firmly, laying her résumé down on the desk, then folding his hands over it, a concerned look on his face. "Are you sure you can handle them, Natalie?" He sat forward abruptly, letting his suddenly dubious gaze go over her slender features. "I have to be honest with you. I've gone through ten nannies in the last ten months. The last one didn't even last a day."

"Why?" Natalie asked in genuine surprise.

A grin slid slowly over his face, softening his features. For a moment he contemplated how much to tell her. Well, in for a penny, in for a pound, he thought. If he wanted her to take care of the boys it was only fair to let her know exactly what she as getting herself into.

"Well, the last nanny went racing out of the house after the boys decided to give Ruth a bath."

Natalie shrugged, confused. "What's wrong with that? Children enjoy giving their pets a bath. Seems like a perfectly fine idea to me."

His grin widened, brightening his eyes and revealing a small, adorable dimple in his chin. "Uh…yeah. Generally I'd agree with you, Natalie. But you see, the boys had the bright idea to give Ruth a bath in the toilet." Jared dragged his hands through his dark hair, hoping she still felt the same way about the job once he finished this explanation. "They knew Ruth wasn't allowed in the bathtub—we'd already had that conversation with another nanny a few months before—so the boys came up with the brilliant idea of dumping half a bottle of liquid dish detergent down the toilet. By flushing repeatedly, they thought for sure they'd get enough bubbles to bathe Ruth properly without disturbing the sanctity of the family bathtub, thus upsetting Mrs. Taylor, our cook and housekeeper, to say nothing of their new nanny, who quit that same day, telling me the boys were incorrigible," he admitted with a wince.

"Incorrigible?" Annoyed at the mere thought of someone labeling her children with such a derogatory term, Natalie all but bristled. "That's utterly ridiculous," she said, with such indignation Jared couldn't help but duck his head to hide a smile. He had a feeling he and Natalie McMahon were going to get along just fine. "They're simply curious little boys. How else are they going to learn about the world if they don't experiment? Incorrigible, indeed!" she finished in a huff.

"Experiment?" he repeated, shaking his head, thoroughly impressed. He laughed in relief. "The boys ended up with enough water and bubbles to float their way to New York, to say nothing of the plumber's bill I had to pay. Not to mention the fact that we lost another nanny." He shrugged, leaning back in his chair again and stretching his cramped, tired legs. "Well, needless to say, that was the tenth nanny in as many months. And so the search has begun anew."

Natalie pushed her hair off her face. "The other nannies simply weren't used to handling young children, especially little boys." Her back was up now at the mere thought that someone had been critical of her children. "I think it's important to let children explore their world—obviously within limits, so that they don't hurt themselves or others. But to label them because they have a naturally curious bent is just as unfair as trying to stifle their natural exuberance."

Jared's grin was huge, and he felt something heavy lift off his shoulders. "Well, Natalie, I have to say your attitude is refreshing, and pretty much in line with mine as far as the boys go." He glanced down at her résumé. "I'm going to have to check your references, of course—"

"Of course." Her heart began to thud in excitement.

"The job comes with room and board, obviously," he added. "This is very much a working ranch, and the ranch is my responsibility and takes up a great deal of my time. We have almost five thousand acres of prime Nevada land. A couple hundred ranch hands live around the property, but you probably won't have much to do with them, or the actual ranching duties. We raise cattle and horses primarily, but we've also got a fairly decent size chicken coop, and a rather large vegetable garden not too far from the house here. We've also got a few other miscellaneous barn animals, Ruth notwithstanding, but your responsibilities will be the boys, and that includes getting them up and dressed for school, packing lunches, chaperoning school field trips, helping with homework and then caring for them after school until dinner. Including some weekends. Most nights we eat about six, unless I've got a big project going on or its birthing season. But otherwise, I'm usually in the house and ready to quit for the day around then. At which point, your time is your own and I'll take over the care of the boys. How does that sound?"

"Can I keep my dog Ditka with me?" she asked hesitantly.

He nodded. "Of course. One more four-legged furry creature won't be a problem."

Natalie wanted to give a huge sigh of relief, but contained herself. "It sounds to me like you work some very long days," she said with a smile.

He shrugged. "It's a rancher's life and I wouldn't have it any other way."

"Well, it sounds wonderful."

Cocking his head, he watched her eyes light up. When she smiled, the sadness left her face and it became almost serene, he realized. Serene and beautiful.

Quickly, he banished the idea, knowing he couldn't allow his thoughts to go anywhere in that direction.

"Now, provided your references check out, how soon can you start?" he asked, not certain he could believe his good fortune.

She frowned a bit. "I've been staying at the Saddle Falls

Hotel in town, so as soon as you check my references, I can pack up my things and start right away.''

''Well, the Saddle Falls Hotel belongs to the Ryans, so I can arrange to have someone bring your things out,'' he said. At her look of surprise, he grinned. ''Our family owns a great many businesses, including this ranch.'' He glanced around at the home he loved, knowing he could never live anywhere else. ''I handle the ranch. Jake, the oldest of my brothers, handles all the real estate acquisitions, and Josh my other brother, who is a lawyer, manages all the Ryan family businesses.''

''Do they all live here?'' she asked, feeling daunted all of a sudden. It had never occurred to her that she might have to deal with Jared Ryan's whole family as well as him.

Jared shook his head. ''No, Jake just got married, and he lives in a smaller house at the back of the ranch with his wife, Rebecca. But they're in Texas right now. My brother Josh mostly stays at his place in town—it's actually a small apartment on the top floor of the hotel. And I, of course, live here on the ranch with the boys. Then there's my grandfather, Tommy Ryan.'' Jared's lips curved. ''Tommy's the patriarch of the family. He's retired now, but still keeps his hand in things so he doesn't get too bored. And, of course, the twins keep him active and busy. He lives here—actually, this is his house. And then there's Mrs. Taylor.''

''Your rather absentminded cook?''

Jared laughed. ''Yes. She has her own suite of rooms at the back of the house, as will you, although yours will be on the other side.'' He frowned suddenly.

''What's wrong?'' Natalie asked with a frown of her own, a frission of alarm racing over her.

"You don't by any chance cook, do you?" he asked, with such hope she couldn't help but laugh.

"Actually, I love to cook." Tilting her head, she studied him with a look akin to suspicion. "Why?"

His mouth quirked at the corners and he tried to contain a smile. "Because Mrs. Taylor is semi-retired and now she only works three days a week, and then only if she feels like it." He shrugged. "She's been with the family since Tommy brought her over from Ireland about nineteen years ago, and is more a part of the family than an employee. But lately she's been a bit absentminded, and I'm a little worried about her growing confusion, working around the stove and all. Until I find a new full-time cook, Mrs. Taylor is it, unless you can help out."

Natalie nodded in understanding. "Well, I can understand your concern, but if she won't mind sharing her kitchen with a stranger, I'd love to take over some of the cooking duties." With a shrug, she smiled. "It's been a long time since I had anyone to cook for, and I think I'd enjoy it."

"Well, we've got plenty of people for you to cook for, and if you can boil hot dogs or make macaroni and cheese, the boys will be in heaven."

"Well, those just happen to be two of my specialties," she said with a laugh, realizing that during the time Jared had been interviewing her, some of the tension had left her, and she'd begun to relax.

"Great." Jared rolled his tired shoulders, wishing for a long, hot shower. But the day wasn't done yet. "I'll tell you what—dinner is just about ready—"

"You hope."

Nodding, he laughed, realizing he was going to enjoy having her around to banter with. "Yes, I hope. Why don't you stay for dinner? I'll grab a quick shower, and you can get better acquainted with the boys. I'd like to tell them you're going to be staying to take care of them, after I check you references, of course. If everything pans out, you can start in the morning."

"That would be wonderful." Relief soared through her and she found all of her muscles growing blessedly relaxed. "And that will give me a chance to try to tackle the 'Lucy the frog-face' problem with the boys before morning," she added.

"Ouch, I almost forgot." He gave that heartbreaking grin. "I have a feeling, Natalie, that you're exactly what the boys need." Pleased, Jared stood up and extended his hand toward her. "Welcome aboard."

She stood up in turn, and he caught a hint of her sweetly feminine scent. It had been so long since he'd smelled anything quite so enticingly female that Jared found himself struggling to fill his lungs with the fragrance, wanting to remember it.

"Thank you, Jared." Her gaze met his, and for a long, silent moment they stared at each other, neither wanting to admit or acknowledge the strength of the feelings coursing though them.

Torn between enjoying her touch, Jared finally broke the contact, realizing that having this beautiful, sensual woman in the house, underfoot everyday, teasing his mind and stirring his senses, was going to be might damn distracting.

Maybe it was about time he followed his brother Josh's advice. Perhaps he did need to get out and socialize with the opposite sex once in a while.

Jared didn't have to make a lifetime commitment, but there was no reason he couldn't simply go out to dinner now and again with a woman.

He'd been so gun-shy the past three years, focusing all

his attention on the boys, the ranch and his family, that he'd denied himself even that small pleasure.

Funny, until today he hadn't realized he'd even missed it.

Nor had he felt particularly lonely.

But for some reason, today he felt a profound sense of loneliness for the opposite sex that he hadn't had in a very long time.

Maybe he *should* think about going out on a date. However, he wondered why the idea of going out with a woman didn't particularly please him—but the thought of perhaps spending more time with Natalie did.

It both pleased and frightened him, he realized.

Frightened him enough to recognize a threat when he saw one, especially in the female form.

Well, he might be a bit lonely, but he wasn't a fool, he thought with a sudden scowl.

He was going to heed the internal warnings and ignore the feelings and emotions Natalie's presence aroused.

For the boys' sake, he told himself.

Definitely for the boys.

After all, they were all that mattered.

# Chapter Three

"Do you like bugs, Natalie?" Terry asked, picking the cheese off the top of his pizza and rolling it into a ball before popping it into his mouth.

"Mmm...bugs?" Natalie repeated absently, as she reached across the dinner table to rescue Terry's glass of milk before it became a casualty of his elbow. "Why?" she asked with a suspicious lift of her brow, shooting an amused glance across the dinner table at Jared, who looked, she realized, dead tired.

But then, in the past few weeks since she'd moved in and taken over care of the boys, he'd often looked exhausted.

She'd had no idea how grueling ranching was, or the hours it required. Her heart went out to Jared when he dragged himself inside the house at night, long after six o'clock the past week or so, totally depleted.

But no matter how tired he was, he still spent at least an hour with the boys. If he missed having dinner with them, he gave them their evening bath. If he missed that, he at least read them a story each night, taking time and care to make sure he gave both boys some individual attention.

And love.

Natalie glanced at Jared now, aware that he'd been looking at her across the table for most of dinner. It made her slightly self-conscious to be the object of his attention. Even when he was exhausted there was no denying his intense masculinity.

The more she was around him, the harder and harder it became to ignore the sizzling spark of awareness that seemed to ignite the moment they were in the same room, or looked at each other.

The other day, they'd accidentally brushed against once another in the kitchen. They both froze as if they'd touched a live wire, staring in stunned silence at each other, as if not quite believing the feelings arcing between them.

Then they'd both judiciously ignored them, simply going about their business as if nothing had happened.

But something *had* happened, and Natalie could no more deny it or ignore it than she could ignore the fact that the more time she spent with Jared, the more she had to accept that he was a wonderful, kind, loving, generous, hardworking man.

She couldn't help but admire him and his commitment to his family, the boys and his responsibilities. But with that admiration came remorse and regret, mixed with a heavy dose of guilt, because she was deliberately deceiving him.

One thing she was absolutely certain of: Jared loved the boys—totally, completely and unconditionally, in a way their own father had never loved them.

Jared was exactly the kind of father she'd always wanted for her sons, the kind of father they deserved. And it made her unbearably sad to know that she was going to have to hurt him.

When the guilt started eating away at her, she reminded herself that the boys were hers, legally, morally and in every other way. But that certainly didn't take away from Jared's love, or the wondrous role he had played in the boys' lives.

Nor did it ease her guilt.

Considering the circumstances, she found herself grateful that her boys had ended up with someone like Jared.

It warmed her heart to know that in her absence, her children had been well-loved, accepted and taken care of by a man who couldn't have loved them more if he'd been their real father. The other possibilities frightened her too much to even think of.

"So, my little lad, what's this about bugs?" Tommy Ryan asked, reaching across the table to help himself to another piece of pizza. His deep, booming voice still carried a lyrical hint of Ireland, and at the moment, a huge dose of humor. Eyes twinkling, Tommy eyed his young grandsons, love radiating from him.

"Billy got a new pet." Terry chomped on his pizza, his cheeks puffed out like a hoarding chipmunk. "And he wants us to keep her while he goes to his grammy's overnight."

"Don't talk with your mouth full, honey," Natalie gently reprimanded, using her own napkin to wipe a smear of tomato sauce from Terry's chin.

Terry made a great show of swallowing, then grinned his toothless grin at her, making Natalie's heart soften. She'd never been happier than she'd been these past few weeks, doing what she'd longed to do for her children, what she'd been denied for three years: taking care of them, nurturing them, loving them, being an integral part of their everyday life.

She couldn't remember ever being happier.

"What kind of a pet?" she asked now with a knowing smile, glancing at Tommy affectionately.

Tommy Ryan had been a bonus she hadn't counted on. He was, in a word, absolutely wonderful—not only totally devoted to the boys, but totally devoted to his family.

And he'd accepted her into their lives with good humor, good grace and a welcoming smile.

When she'd first arrived, it was Tommy who had been home during the day with her, Tommy who had done his level best to make her feel welcome and at ease.

She utterly adored Tommy Ryan.

And he, too, was going to be hurt by her deception.

The thought made her stomach roil, and deliberately, she pushed it away, forcing herself to concentrate on what Terry was saying.

"It's a girl pet," he said with a barely concealed snarl. "Her name's Matilda."

Tommy nodded, eyes glinting with amusement. "Matilda, now that's a fine, fine name, lad."

"Son..." Jared leaned forward, trying not to look amused as he fingered his coffee cup, but knowing the twins well enough to sense there was far more to this than Terry was letting on. "Exactly what *is* Matilda?" he asked pointedly.

Terry glanced at his brother, and they exchanged sheepish looks.

"What?" Natalie glanced from the boys to Jared, and then Tommy. All four males wore identical "gotcha" expressions, making her suddenly wary. She swallowed hard, knowing she was probably going to regret it, but asking anyway. "What is Matilda?" Her gaze shifted from Terry to Timmy, who immediately ducked his head behind his slice of pizza to hide a grin. "An orangutan or something?" she asked. Jared had not been lying when he told her the twins were adventuresome. She'd come to learn they were all of that—and more.

Terry shrugged. "A stupid girl spider, but she's cool, anyway." He stuffed another piece of pizza in his mouth, then grinned.

"A spider," Natalie said carefully. "And Billy wants us to, what? Spider sit Matilda while he's at his grandmother's?" Her voice crept up a bit in shock.

"Yup." Terry's mop of black hair flopped in his eyes as he shook his head. "His grandma likes lizards."

"Well, that is something to be grateful for, I suppose." Natalie took a sip of her soft drink. "And so what does Billy's grandmother liking lizards have to do with us watching Matilda?"

Jared grinned at her, giving her a thumbs-up. She was learning that the boys had a special talent not just for mischief but for roping adults in with half stories. It was just another thing that impressed the hell out of him about Natalie and the way she'd taken over the care of the boys. She was a natural.

"Well..." Terry began slowly, "Billy's grandma said he could bring his lizard collection—"

"*Collection?*" Natalie all but croaked, nearly choking on her soft drink. "Billy has a collection of lizards?"

"Course." Terry shrugged, eyeing the remaining pizza. "It's not a real collection, though, only about six or seven."

"Is that all?" Natalie murmured wryly.

"And, well, Billy's grandma doesn't like spiders."

"Well, at least Billy's grandma and I have something in common."

"What?" Terry eyed her owlishly. "Do your teeth come out at night, too?" he asked with a giggle.

Natalie laughed. "No, sweetheart, I'm sorry, my teeth don't come out. But I'm not real fond of lizards, either," she admitted.

"Why?" Terry was looking at her as if he couldn't even comprehend the idea.

"Why?" Natalie blew out a breath, then glanced at Jared, hoping for some help. He just grinned at her. Apparently there'd be no help forthcoming from him. "Well, they're slimy and creepy, and they slither all over the place." She could barely suppress a shudder.

"Yeah, isn't it great?" Grinning from ear to ear, Timmy reached for another piece of pizza.

"Terrific," Natalie said without much enthusiasm.

"Son, why don't you tell Natalie exactly what Billy's grandmother liking lizards but not spiders has to do with us?"

"Oh." Terry reached for his milk, gulped it, then set it back down on the table. He went to wipe his milk mustache off his mouth with his sleeve, but caught the look Natalie sent him, and grinned sheepishly, reaching for his napkin. "Well, Matilda's a tarantula—"

"Oh my word!" Horrified, Natalie grabbed the edge of the table. "Matilda's a *what?*"

Terry looked at his dad as if to ask "What did I say?" Then he turned to Natalie with a shrug. "A tarantula," he repeated nonchalantly, shrugging his slender, bony shoulders again. "And she's cute, even if she is a girl," he added with an animated scowl.

"Cute," Natalie repeated. She shook her head. "How on earth can a tarantula be cute?" She scowled in turn. "And aren't they dangerous?" Her curious glance encompassed the whole table.

"Nay, lassie, tarantulas may look fierce, but they're as harmless as lambs." Reaching across the table, Tommy gave her hand a comforting pat. "Unless you corner or frighten one, they're harmless."

"Harmless?" she repeated dully, not certain any spider was harmless.

"Aye, lassie." Tommy gave her hand another pat. "I promise."

Taking a deep breath, Natalie nodded. "Okay, Terry, so tell me, what did you say to Billy when he asked if we'd keep Matilda for him while he went to his grandmother's?" She was heartily certain she was *not* going to like his answer.

"Nuthin'." He shoveled the last of his piece of pizza into his mouth. "Told him I had to ask you first," he said, chomping loudly.

Pleased, touched and surprised, Natalie glanced at Jared. There was warmth and love shining in his eyes as he looked at Terry, and she felt her heart tumble over. The man adored her children, so much it almost broke her heart. She glanced at Terry, felt tears burn the back of her eyes.

"Oh, sweetheart," she said softly, getting up to enfold Terry in a hug, brushing a hand through his silky hair and giving him a quick peck on the cheek before he started squirming and getting embarrassed at being hugged in front of everyone. "Thank you. That was very sweet of you," she said softly, stroking her hand over his head again.

"Yes, Son." Jared beamed at Terry. "And very thoughtful to consider Natalie's feelings." His gaze shifted to her again, and he felt that familiar bump in his heart he had come to associate with Natalie, only with Natalie.

In the past few weeks, having her in his life, he'd found himself thinking, daydreaming, wishing—wanting things he had no business wanting.

At first he'd thought he was just lonely, starved for a woman's companionship, but now he realized it went way beyond that. There was a warmth of awareness between them, some kind of emotional connection he simply couldn't explain. He'd thought it was simply because they were so in tune about the boys. Their outlook on raising children, setting limits and boundaries, the way the boys should behave, the values he thought the boys should learn—he and Natalie shared all the same beliefs, which made leaving them in her care so much easier, and eased his own guilt at not being able to spend all his time with them.

His initial skepticism about her had given way to admiration very quickly. And something more.

She lavished love, attention and affection on the boys, and they were blossoming under her expert tutelage. She had those very rare qualities of patience, kindness and definitely a sense of humor, all things he'd always thought necessary for a mother.

*Mother.*

The thought came unbidden, surprising him, and Jared felt a flash of guilt. Natalie had quickly become the mother he'd always wished Kathryn had been, the mother his precious boys had always deserved but had never had.

He no longer worried about the twins when they were with Natalie. She'd lifted the burden of pain and guilt from his shoulders and his heart, so that he could now go through his daily life, knowing with absolute certainty his boys were happy, healthy, safe and, more importantly, loved.

But in the past few weeks, he was beginning to realize that the unusual, intense emotional connection that seemed to link him and Natalie, was due to a lot more than the boys.

Jared could no longer deny the impact Natalie was having on him and his wary, scared, scarred heart.

She was so honest, so genuine, that she allowed him to drop all the barriers he'd erected in order to defend himself.

He didn't feel the need to protect himself from Natalie.

As such, his feelings seemed to spring to life, escaping from the barren outpost he'd banished them to.

Looking at her now, he felt desire sweep over him, along with something else—admiration.

Their gazes met, clung, and Jared felt that strong yearning flare to life. A yearning to make her his.

It was getting stronger and stronger.

In the weeks since he'd hired her, Natalie had become not only important in the boys' lives, but an integral part of the family. Even Tommy adored her.

She'd become *necessary,* Jared thought, not for the first time. She'd become a necessary and much needed part of their existence.

His brows drew together and he realized a bit absently that sometime during the past weeks, Natalie had unwittingly become an integral part of his life as well—even if she didn't know it.

For the first time in years, he had to admit he found himself looking forward to coming home at night, knowing she'd be there. He'd grown accustomed to seeing her first thing in the morning, scrambling around the kitchen, preparing the boys' breakfast, making their lunches, getting them ready for school, doing all the things Kathryn had never taken time nor wanted to do.

Jared had no idea how or when he'd started considering Natalie in a way that had nothing to do with her caretaking duties. He'd found himself dreaming about her at night, and thinking about her during the day. Even when she wasn't near, he could recall her sweetly sensual scent or see her beautiful, smiling face.

He'd been deeply concerned by his growing feelings, and in an effort to keep things in perspective, had deliberately avoided her except when absolutely necessary, or when his grandfather or the boys were around.

Like tonight.

He'd been coming back to the house later and later each evening, hoping to avoid her, and to avoid another sleepless night thinking about her. So he wore himself out with physical labor during the day, only to discover his mental labor at night—thinking about her—kept him awake, anyway.

He'd forced himself into exile from females out of need and fear. The need to protect himself and the fear that he couldn't or wouldn't be able to do so.

And so now, faced with the prospect of a beautiful, delightful woman who made his children hugely happy, and brought some much needed joy to his own life, Jared found himself questioning his growing feelings toward her.

So he'd simply avoided being alone with her.

If she noticed, or if it bothered her, she never said a word about it. Not that he was surprised. Natalie McMahon had not taken one misstep.

He was just lonely, he'd told himself on more than one occasion. And impressed with how well she was handling the children. Nothing more.

Glancing across the dinner table at her now, he realized that she was exactly the kind of woman he'd always thought a wife and a mother should be. The thought shook him all the way to his boots.

*Wife.*

Where had that come from? he wondered grimly. He hadn't even thought the word, much less said it, in over three years. He couldn't afford to even be thinking along those lines, he realized, shifting his gaze to the boys.

He couldn't afford to be foolish, couldn't afford to ever take a chance on another woman.

For their sake.

As it was, the boys were growing attached to Natalie, more so than he'd ever believed possible. But then again, they'd never been exposed to a nanny this long before, simply because none had even made it this far.

But Natalie had.

His gaze shifted back to her, and he watched her engage in animated conversation with Timmy, all the while keeping an eye on Terry, who was trying to shovel another piece of pizza—whole—into his mouth. Jared bit back a grin.

Without taking her attention off of Timmy or their conversation, she effortlessly retrieved Terry's pizza, cut it into bite-size pieces, then slid his plate back to him.

Jared didn't know why, but her actions both annoyed and impressed the hell out of him.

He blew out a breath. He needed some time alone, some time to get his thoughts and feelings in perspective. Some time away from Natalie.

He pushed back from the table and stood up. "Sorry to eat and run, but I've got to go check on that new Hereford bull. He was a bit too antsy for my tastes this afternoon."

"Jared?" Natalie's voice stopped him midstep, and reluctantly, he turned to her, wanting only to escape from the kitchen, and his own thoughts about her, as quickly as possible.

"Would you mind if I walked out with you?" She glanced at Tommy. "Could you keep an eye on the twins until I get back? I need to talk to Jared about something."

"Happy to, lass," Tommy said with a smile. "It's not often I get the full attention of these two handsome, strapping lads all to myself." He turned to the boys. "How about if Grandpop gives you your baths?"

"Yeah!" they caroled in unison.

"Granpop lets us splash all we want." Terry scrambled down from the chair, nearly toppling it in the process.

"Yeah, and he doesn't care if we get the floor wet," Timmy added.

"Well, I do," Natalie admonished with a laugh, as she reached for her jacket off the peg near the back door. "And Ruth may *not* take a bath with you," she added for good measure, seeing the gleam in Terry's eye.

She followed Jared out into the darkness, shutting the back door softly behind her, then slipping her arms into her jacket. Saying nothing, Jared walked beside her, pausing to help her with her jacket. His fingers brushed against the silky softness of the hair at her nape and he felt the jolt of yearning, of longing all the way through his system. He yanked his fingers back as if he'd been burned.

Annoyed at himself, he stuffed his hands in his jacket pockets and continued walking, trying to turn his thoughts to something—anything—else.

"Nights are getting cooler." He glanced up at the sky, which was midnight blue, with a few twinkling stars. He wanted to look anywhere but at her. "Pretty soon fall will be well under way." He wasn't much for small talk, but at the moment, he was as nervous as a fifteen-year-old on his first date. Natalie made him feel that way—clumsy, tongue-tied and just a little bit desperate.

"It's so beautiful out here," she commented, glancing at the sky as well. "So different from Chicago." She shivered in spite of her jacket. "By this time in October, it would have turned almost bitterly cold, with high winds and driving rains." She shivered again just thinking about it. "I think I much prefer the weather in Nevada."

"You do?" He made the mistake of looking down at her. She was gazing up at him, and with her face bathed in starlight, he could see how beautiful she was.

Her mouth, that luscious mouth he'd thought about so many, many times, was far too intriguing. The ache in his belly grew, then slid lower, causing him to turn away from her without a word and keep walking.

"Have I done something to upset you?" she asked quietly, surprising him.

He turned back to her, his look concerned. "Of course not. Why on earth would you think that?"

She shrugged, but kept walking, trying to keep her pace even with his. "I'm not sure. You've just seemed a bit cool the past week or so."

He didn't trust himself to look at her, fearing he'd reach out and touch her, something he knew he couldn't allow. No matter how much he wanted it—craved it. "No, I'm just very busy and preoccupied, worried about a lot of things."

"And are the boys one of those things?" she asked softly, glancing at him again.

Surprised, he paused once more, wondering why he'd never noticed just how small and fragile she was.

"No," he said with a breath of relief. "The boys are not one of the things I'm worried about." He managed a smile. "At least I haven't worried about them since I hired you." He hesitated, then flipped the collar of her jacket down, giving in to temptation and letting his fingers linger there, feeling the roughness of the denim against his fingertips, wishing instead it was the softness of her skin. "You've done a wonderful job with them, Natalie. I've never seen them take to someone, especially a woman, so quickly. You have a definite talent with children and I'm sorry I haven't taken the time to tell you that before."

Pleased, she smiled up at him. "Thanks, but they are a joy, and I love being with them every day." She hesitated, licked her lips, then went on. "You know, Jared, you've done a remarkable job with them, single parent or not. The boys haven't lacked for anything." He had given them a very solid foundation, and for that, she would always be grateful.

"Thanks." He knew he couldn't keep looking at her face, that mouth that was too close, too inviting. "You said you wanted to talk to me about something?" He wanted to get this over with. Being with her was just too hard on him. He didn't trust the way she made him feel, the things she made him want, need.

"Yes, Halloween is in a few weeks, and I was wondering if it would be all right if the boys had a Halloween party and invited all their friends over."

He frowned a bit. This wasn't something she had to ask him while they were alone; she could have asked him in the house. "Of course," he said, slightly confused. "I'm sure they'd love it. But are you sure you can handle even more kids? Seems to me the twins would be more than enough for any woman."

She laughed. "Well, they are, but Timmy's having a bit of a problem in school—"

"What kind of a problem?" Jared asked, instantly alert.

She reached up and placed her hands on his chest in comfort. "Oh, Jared, I'm sorry. I didn't mean to alarm you." She could feel the rapid beating of his heart beneath her palms, and instantly felt contrite for worrying him. "It's nothing serious, I assure you. But Timmy's just having a bit of trouble right now. I went to school yesterday to see his teacher."

"And?" Worry crept into his voice.

Natalie sighed. "And apparently Timmy's been having

some difficulty with his spelling. I've been working with him after school, and he's learned the whole alphabet, but he's apparently having trouble printing letters.'' She glanced up at Jared with a smile, then froze. She hadn't realized how close they were standing to each other, hadn't realized her hands were on his chest, and that his had somehow slipped to her waist.

Natalie's heart started to pound, and she felt her throat go dry. Being this close to him made her so vividly aware of him that she wasn't certain she could continue. With great effort, she tried to gather her thoughts. ''Anyway, he's printing some of his letters backward.''

''Backward?'' Jared asked in confusion. ''But isn't that pretty normal for a little kid?''

''Sometimes,'' she said carefully. ''But that's not the main problem.'' She licked her lips again, then shivered as the wind kicked up, chilly and brisk, cutting through her leggings and T-shirt. Jared's hands instinctively tightened around her, drawing her closer to his warmth.

''What is the main problem?''

''Some of the other kids are making fun of him, giving him a hard time about the problems he's having. I guess last week the teacher called on him to write a word on the board, and he printed some letters backward so the kids couldn't read it.''

Shaking his head, Jared sighed. ''Some things never change. Kids can be horrible to one another, can't they?''

''Definitely.'' Looking into his eyes played havoc with her system, so she lowered her gaze to stare at the buttons on his shirt. ''So I thought maybe if the boys had a party—''

''And invited the kids who are making fun of Timmy, it might smooth the way for him a bit?''

Her gaze shot to his in surprise, and she laughed. The

sound drifted through the quiet night air. "How did you know?"

Everything inside of him warmed and his heart turned over. Her caring for his sons touched him in a way nothing had in a long, long time, and he couldn't prevent the feelings that moved over him like a steamroller, flattening every warning.

"Oh, Natalie." Instinct took over as well as need, and he drew her against him for a hug. He was surprised she was so light, so delicate. She fit perfectly, her head resting right under his chin as if she were made for him. "I knew because my mother did the same thing for my brother Josh when we were kids." He drew back and glanced down at her. "Of course, Jake and I wanted to handle it our own way."

Lifting her head from the safety and comfort of his chest, realizing she was enjoying their closeness, she asked, "Let me guess. With your fists?"

"You got it," he admitted with a grin. "You pick on one Ryan, you'll end up taking on them all."

"Well, Jared, I'm not exactly experienced with my fists, so I thought a Halloween party might do the trick."

"It might," he admitted, still smiling. Their eyes met and held. Unable to resist, Jared lifted a hand to her cheek. "Natalie…" His voice was a whisper in the darkness, touching her heart, filling it with longing. "I don't know how to tell you—what to say—to explain how much you've come to mean to…the boys." He didn't want to talk; he simply wanted to kiss her, to press his lips to hers, to hold her softness against him to ease this aching need tearing through him.

Nestling her face against the warmth and tenderness of his hand, Natalie allowed her eyes to close, let herself enjoy for just this one, brief moment the luxury of Jared's touch.

Until this moment, she hadn't realized how much she'd wanted Jared to touch her, how much she needed to feel him close.

Jared Ryan had touched her on levels she'd never believed possible, had never experienced before, certainly not with a man.

She'd never felt this kind of connection with anyone until now. It was foreign, frightening, and yet exciting.

"Nat?"

Her eyes fluttered open and she looked up at him. Emotions thickened the air between them, and for a moment they merely stared into each other's eyes, wanting, needing, yearning.

"Nat." Her name came out a soft groan before Jared gave in to the urge and slowly lowered his mouth to hers. He saw her eyes widen, felt her hands clench into fists on his jacket as she realized his intent.

For an instant, he saw fear in her eyes, and almost stopped, but then his lips touched hers.

It was like coming home.

A riot of feelings and needs erupted, nearly knocking the breath from him. She tasted of magic and moonlight and a bevy of mysterious things he'd denied himself for so very, very long.

And he only knew that he wanted—needed—more.

Tightening his arms around her, he drew her even closer to him, until her softness was pressed the full length of his aching body. His mouth slowly, gently seduced hers, feasting on what he had only imagined, dreamed about until now.

The dream didn't come close to the pleasure of this reality.

He groaned when her arms tightened around his neck, her fingers sliding into his hair. Her touch set off sparks of fire, making him press his body closer to hers, wanting, needing to quench the flames of desire that had been building since the moment he'd laid eyes on her.

His hands ached with the need to touch more of her, to feel the soft roundness of her breasts, the tightened peak of her nipple. He groaned again, pulling her closer until she was on tiptoe, clinging to him, returning all the passion that poured out of him.

Natalie clung to Jared, feeling as if the world had tilted and she would fall off if she didn't hold on to him. She'd never experienced this kind of breath-stealing, gut-wrenching passion before. Had never known that one kiss, one embrace could send her world spinning off its axis.

She wanted more.

The thought screamed through her, making her arch against him, wanting to ease the ache she felt in every inch of her being. Making her want Jared in a way she'd never wanted another man.

When she felt his fingers slide through her hair, angling her head for better purchase, she made no protest, merely snuggled closer to his warmth, his hardness, wanting only to be nearer to him.

Being in Jared's arms was like coming home, she thought hazily. They fit together perfectly—like two puzzle pieces that had finally found their rightful place.

Luxuriating in Jared's arms, in the feelings he'd evoked, Natalie realized how dangerous these emotions were, how dangerous the situation was.

She couldn't allow herself to be swept away like this. If she did, it might affect her her sons.

Reality hit her like a bucket of cold water, and she moaned softly, in sorrow and regret, before slowly drawing back from him. Weak-kneed, she let her head drop against his chest for a moment, trying to get her breath, unfog her brain.

He simply held her close, his hands stroking her back, letting her know he was there, holding her, comforting her.

Oh, how she wanted to simply give in and accept what he was offering. She'd come to know him well enough to know Jared was not a man who trifled with feelings—not his or anyone else's.

He was solid, dependable. The kind of man any woman—well, any woman in her right mind—would want.

Except her.

Natalie couldn't want him.

She knew that, but at the moment, she was having trouble accepting it.

"You okay?" he asked softly, his hands still stroking her back. She was trembling against him, and he wasn't certain if it was from passion or the cold.

"Yeah." Natalie blew out a breath and took a step back, knowing if she didn't right now she might not be able to. The comfort of Jared's arms was far too tempting.

"Should I apologize?"

It was the first time she'd ever sensed even a chink in his confidence, and it touched her deeply.

"No, Jared." She looked at him, saw the darkness of desire in his eyes, and felt more remorse than she'd ever felt in her life. Men like Jared Ryan were rare; she'd never come across anyone like him before, and under any other circumstances, she could easily fall in love with him. The thought terrified her. "Don't apologize. Don't be sorry." She didn't think she could handle that. Even though she knew she couldn't allow this to continue, or to go any further, she truly wasn't sorry it had happened.

She had wondered what it would be like to kiss Jared.

Now she knew.

And that knowledge would have to be enough, for it was all she would ever have, she thought sadly, looking up into his beautiful eyes.

"Nat." He touched her cheek again. He'd heard the pain in her voice, the uncertainty, and knew that he *should* regret kissing her, *should* apologize. but he didn't regret it, and in fact, wanted to do it again.

"I'd better go in." She drew back from him, pulling her jacket tighter. Somehow the night seemed colder and darker.

Jared dropped his arms from her waist. "Good night, Nat." He wanted to touch her, to kiss her again, to hold her in his arms until the sadness in her eyes was replaced by something far more suitable to her.

"Night." She turned and headed back toward the house, knowing he was watching her, feeling the warmth of his gaze on her back. She was sorely tempted to turn, race back to him and throw herself into his arms, but she didn't, couldn't.

But she did turn to look at him one last time before she slipped inside. One last glance that made her heart ache.

# Chapter Four

"Well, Lassie, looks to me like you've had quite a time of it." Tommy Ryan stood in doorway of the living room with an amused smile on his face. Grinning, he started across the room toward her, leaning heavily on his elegant, hand carved cane.

In spite of a bad hip, at eighty, Tommy Ryan still had the large, powerful build of the boxer he had once been, a build that had intimidated more than its fair share of stout men over the years.

Age and infirmary had not stooped his frame, but merely slowly his gait. His hair, which had once been a thick, mane of coal in his youth, was now a thick shock of white framing his face like an elegant halo. His skin was a rich, deep tan, lined with the experience and memories of his long life.

His mouth was full and firm and more often than not curved into a grin, as if he had a secret he wasn't quite ready to share with the world yet. His blue eyes, the color of the deepest sapphires still twinkled with mischief most of the time, giving him the appearance of a slightly naughty, oversized leprechaun.

There was an air of power and authority radiating from him, the kind that only very successful men possess.

He was a man who'd been blessed with more luck than any man deserved, more money then he could ever hope to spend, and a family he adored more than life itself.

But interspersed in the joys of his life had been sorrow. A deep, aching sorrow that no amount of joy could erase.

Surveying the damage in his living room, he was carried back in time to when his grandsons were boys, and they'd had their fair share of parties.

*Jesse.*

The thought came unbidden, as it always did, taking him by surprise, catching him off guard. Even after all these years he felt a stab in his heart as sharp as a saber when he thought of his youngest grandson. Gone all these years, but aye, never forgotten. Not for a moment, not for a day.

*Twenty years.*

He shut his eyes in remembrance and remorse. Jesse had missed so much, he thought sadly, hearing the echoes of long-ago laughter. It was so real that for a moment Tommy wondered if perhaps he *had* been thrown back in time.

His eyes fluttered open and he glanced around. Watching Jared's mischievous young twins reminded him all too often of the mischief his own grandsons had gotten into, and all too acutely of his loss.

As time passed, that loss seemed to deepen. Perhaps it was just that he knew his time was growing short, and he wasn't certain he could meet his maker until he knew for sure what had happened to his beloved youngest grandson.

*Jesse,* he thought again, biting back a sigh. Aye, how he missed the lad. Jesse would be almost twenty-five now, a grown man, perhaps with babes of his own.

"Tommy," Natalie moaned, rousing him out of his reverie. "I surrender. Unconditionally. I'd wave a white flag but I don't have the energy to lift my hand." From the couch, Natalie moaned and rolled over, looking at him through eyes blurry with fatigue. "I hate to admit it, Tommy, but I've been done in by ten tiny men disguised as five-year-olds." Barely suppressing a shudder, Natalie tried to sit up. She simply couldn't manage it, so let her head flop back down, and closed her eyes.

She couldn't bear to survey the damage to the living room, anyway. Not yet. She'd barely survived looking at the kitchen.

She figured by the time the boys were ready for high school, she might be able to get the last of the ice cream off the walls, and with a little help, perhaps she could salvage the wood floor in the kitchen, although she might need a blowtorch to do it. The curtains covering the patio doors were a lost cause; even she knew that.

Before doing a complete inventory of the day's damage, she figured she needed a couple of aspirin and a few moment's rest, if only to gather her courage.

And her strength.

"Aye, I can see that, lass," Tommy said with a grin, surveying the scene in amusement. "'Twas the boys' Halloween party today, if I recall?"

"Party?" Natalie forced herself up, groaning as her muscles protested. She glanced down with a frown at her once pristine white shirt, which was now smeared with ice cream, chocolate syrup and a dollop of chunky peanut butter. "It wasn't a party, Tommy, it was an ambush. And I lost." Her eyes rounded suddenly. "Tommy, watch where you walk," she cautioned, causing him to stop midstep. "Billy brought his lizard collection to the party. One went

AWOL." Shaking her head in disbelief, she stifled a yawn. "He's still among the missing."

"Lizards, you say?" Tommy said, trying not to grin as he picked his way over the debris scattered across the living room floor. "Hmm, Billy's always been an interesting lad, as I recall."

"Interesting?" Natalie paused, pushing her tangled hair off her face and suppressing a shudder. "That would be a word for it. Not quite the word I'd use…" Her voice trailed off and she lifted her bare feet to the couch, hugging her knees tightly. "And then, of course, there was his other pet." Scowling, she scanned the floor with suspicion, grateful her bare feet were safely tucked under her.

"Other pet, lass?" Tommy asked with a curious lift of his brow.

"An eight-legged creature wearing a brown fur coat." Rubbing her aching forehead, Natalie glanced around suspiciously again. "Matilda's not use to crowds, and she apparently got scared." Natalie managed a weak smile. "She broke for daylight." Natalie shuddered again, remembering the squeals and screams—hers—when she realized Billy's pet spider was on the loose in the house. Her gaze softened and she shrugged. "And then of course, Ditka and Ruth had to get into the act, chasing and scrambling and barking after the poor thing, and then the boys started chasing the dogs—" Natalie broke off, shaking her head, remembering the mayhem and madness. She laughed suddenly, shoving her hair off her face again. "I'm surprised we didn't break some county noise code or something."

Tommy laughed as well. "Sounds like you had a fine time, indeed, lass." From the glowing look on her face, he wondered who'd had a better time at the party, the children or her. It would be a toss-up, he decided, pleased.

"I promised Terry we'd find Matilda and no one would

step on her." She dragged a hand through her hair. "Obviously I was delirious by that time."

"Obviously," Tommy said with some sympathy, glancing at the floor to see if Matilda was about. "And Matilda would be Billy's pet tarantula?" he asked with a knowing smile, making Natalie groan. "The one his grandmother's not overly fond of?"

"That would be the same one." Suppressing a shudder, Natalie pressed a hand to her forehead, which had begun to thud like a bongo drum. "Let's just hope there are no others." The mere thought of the wicked-looking, eight-legged, furry creature was enough to send her up onto the nearest table.

"But they're harmless, lass—you know that, don't you? Tarantulas may be fierce looking, but they truly are harmless."

"That's what people told me about little boys," she said with a scowl, hugging her legs tighter. "After today, you can't fool me. I know the truth."

"Aye, I'll bet you do, lass." Tommy laughed, extending his hand to her to help her from the couch. "I'll bet you do. But you've done a fine, fine job, and I'm sure the boys had a memorable time."

She smiled, taking his hand, allowing him to help her up even if every muscle protested. She wasn't accustomed to chasing ten five-year-olds, two dogs and numerous slithering, crawling, creeping creatures around for three hours. "They had a ball, Tommy," she said, her eyes glowing in remembered pleasure. "Timmy said it was the best Halloween they've ever had."

"Aye, I've no doubt of that." The elderly man gave a pleased nod, glancing around at the shambles that was once the living room. It wouldn't take too long to put it to rights again, he hoped. "And I'm sure 'twill ease the way for the

lad a bit.'' Eyes glimmering, he gave her a knowing smile.
"You've a way with them, lass, you know that?'' His head
bobbed. "Aye, a special way. They're flourishing.'' He
gave her hand a gentle squeeze. "You've brought love to
this house again.'' His gaze softened with affection. "It's
been missing a long time,'' he added, "and I can't thank
you enough, lassie.'' Lifting her hand, he kissed it, warming her heart. "Not nearly enough, indeed.''

Contrite over her deception, Natalie clung to his hand. It
was warm and comforting, much the way her father's had
been. "Oh, Tommy, you don't have to thank me. I love
them.'' The simple words came from her heart and were
filled with aching emotion.

"Aye, I know that, lass,'' he said quietly, carefully,
studying her face. "The love you feel, it's in your gaze
when you look at the imps, in your voice when you talk to
them. Aye, it's clear to anyone with eyes that you couldn't
love them more if they were your own.'' He looked past
her toward something only he could see. "And it's a special
woman who can love children not born of her, lass,'' he
said quietly. "Aye, a special woman, indeed.''

The soft hint of sadness in his voice had her glancing at
him and feeling her own heart ache. She knew she was on
dangerous ground here, and had to be doubly careful. She'd
come to adore Tommy in the same way she'd once adored
her own father. Lying to Tommy, deceiving him, was so
painful, she could almost feel a physical ache. Deliberately,
she steered the conversation away from herself.

"You're talking about Jared's wife, Kathryn, aren't
you?'' she asked quietly. Although she and Tommy had
discussed numerous things since she'd arrived, they had
studiously avoided talking about Jared's marriage. On top
of everything else, she didn't want to seem as if she were
prying.

What Tommy valued was his family, his home. And she absolutely adored him.

Perhaps that's why they'd become such instant friends and so close. She felt a comfort with Tommy she hadn't felt since her father's death.

And she knew she was playing a dangerous game with people's emotions.

She hoped that once the truth came out, once she had to tell them who she really was and why she was there, they'd be able to understand. And forgive her.

"Aye, I guess I am talking of Kathryn," Tommy said with a soft sigh, turning to her with a smile. He hadn't seen his grandson smile so much, or look so happy, in years, not since before Kathryn had left. Tommy had thought for certain the woman had frozen Jared's heart with her coldness and cruelty, but now, since Natalie had arrived, he had hope that Jared would one day find love.

And Natalie would be a fine, fine choice, he'd decided within days of meeting her. She was a beautiful, kind, lovely lass with a loving heart and a generous spirit. She'd taken the twins into her heart, giving them all the attention and affection the young lads had been missing for so long. Tommy admired the lass in a way he hadn't admired a woman in a long time. And his opinion had only grown stronger in the two months since Natalie had arrived.

The only thing that troubled him was the sadness in her eyes. Only one who'd known the loss of a loved one, the deep, aching sadness, could recognize it in another, and he recognized it in Natalie. Although curious, he wouldn't pry. Nay, it wasn't his way. If and when she was ready to talk of the shadow that stalked her, he'd be there to listen, and hopefully to ease the burden that weighed heavily on her slender shoulders.

Now if he could just get his grandson to stop being such

a stubborn, blind dunderhead, and realize what a jewel Natalie was—not just as a woman, but as a potential wife, and especially as a mother—well then, perhaps things could move forward.

He'd have to get to work on it, Tommy decided. If his grandson was too blind to see what was good for him, well then, he'd just have to take matters into his own hands. After all, he was the patriarch of the Ryan clan. It was not only his right, but his responsibility to see that his boys were married proper.

Tommy smiled to himself, remembering when he'd tried that line on his eldest grandson, Jake. It was a wonder his ears weren't still blistered. But at least Jake, in the end, had seen that the lovely Rebecca was indeed right for him, even if it had taken the boy a month of Sundays to figure it out. Tommy wanted to shake his head. He could only hope Jared would eventually see the light, too.

"Some women just aren't cut out for mothering," Natalie said simply, groping for something to say about Kathryn that would hide her true feelings about the woman's abandonment of Jared and the boys. It was both inconceivable and despicable.

"True enough, I suppose," Tommy said quietly, his rubber-tipped cane clicking softly on the ceramic tile as he continued to lead her down the hall. "But then again, some women are born to mothering—like you." He smiled down at her and she glanced away, feeling a pang of guilt.

Although she and Tommy had discussed numerous things in the past weeks since she'd arrived, not once had he mentioned Kathryn by name.

Nor had Jared. And Natalie had to admit she was curious about the woman, and just a bit jealous. Kathryn had had everything Natalie always wanted, but had never been fortunate to have: two beautiful children, a loving husband and a big, extended family who loved and accepted her.

How could she have simply walked away from it all?

Natalie mentally shook her head. Several times she'd almost asked Jared about her, but had caught herself just in time. Things had changed between them since the night he'd kissed her, but not so much that she felt comfortable prying into his personal life, especially when it was clear he wasn't comfortable talking about it. But then again, there were a lot of things she wasn't comfortable about, so they steadfastly danced around the very personal subjects, which suited her fine.

It allowed her to just relax and enjoy Jared's company without worrying or watching every word she said, and she found, to her surprise, that she and Jared got along wonderfully, had a lot in common and could discuss any number of subjects with ease.

Now, each evening while he read the boys their bedtime story, she'd wait for him in the kitchen. Then they'd sit together and enjoy a cup of coffee while they talked about the day. At first they'd met together on the premise of discussing the boys' antics, but it soon evolved into something more substantial. Natalie hated to admit she'd come to look forward to that time each day, when she would see Jared and be alone with him.

"Now, lass, you've put in a day," Tommy said, pausing outside her bedroom door. "I think you deserve an evening off. It will be your first since you arrived, I think."

An evening off? The thought brought on a momentary bout of panic. She had no idea what she'd do with herself with a whole night free. Almost every waking moment since she'd arrived had been spent with the twins.

"But what about the boys?" Dusk had fallen, the day's trick-or-treating was done, the party was over. But she still had responsibilities. Dinner to make. A spelling quiz to go over. She frowned. ''There're things that still need to be done.''

''Aye, I'm certain of it, lass, but they'll get done with or without you on this night.'' Tommy opened her bedroom door and urged her forward. ''Now, your time is your own tonight. Take a long, hot bubble bath, read a book, take a nap.''

They all sounded positively heavenly. And decadent.

''Do whatever strikes your fancy, lass. You've a whole evening to indulge yourself.'' He touched her cheek. ''You've earned it.''

''But what about dinner?'' she asked, her mind spinning with all the things that needed to be handled. With two little boys around, there was always something that had to be done. ''I haven't prepared anything for dinner yet, but I can whip something up for you.''

Shaking his head, Tommy laughed. She was as stubborn and responsible as his grandson. They'd make a fine match. ''Lass, if I can't convince Mrs. Taylor to rustle something up, I think I can manage to burn some meat on that grill my grandson has parked out on the patio.'' He nudged her forward. ''It's not your worry. For tonight, I want you to simply relax.'' He kissed her cheek. ''You've more than earned it.'' He laughed. ''Along with hazardous-duty pay for this day.''

Weakening, Natalie smiled in gratitude. The idea of a hot bubble bath and a nap sounded blissful, and she knew her aching muscles would thank her.

''Thanks, Tommy. I appreciate it. But call me if you change your mind about dinner.'' With a sigh, she went into her own blissfully quiet, clean room, and shut the door behind her, leaning wearily against it. Then, remembering

Matilda, she scurried into the bathroom to run her bath and retrieve her slippers.

"Natalie." Sitting on the edge of her bed in the shadows, Jared gently touched her cheek.

She was curled on her side, hands under her head, sleeping soundly. The pristine white sheet was tucked under her arm, revealing just a hint of the curve of her breast. With some effort, he averted his gaze, trying not to think of the wisp of white silk caressing her gentle curves.

Her dark hair was spread across the pillow like a silken halo, emphasizing the delicate bone structure of her face, those beautiful eyes, the lush, gentle curve of her lips.

The scent of her bath oil hovered in the air, enticing and intoxicating him, making his stomach clench as desire clawed at him.

He'd come home a little over an hour ago to find Tommy knee-deep in debris from the party, and the boys bubbling over with tales about their day.

It had been, Timmy announced, the best day of his life.

The twins had launched themselves at Jared, climbing up his legs, anxious to tell about their Halloween adventures. He'd sat down on the couch—in something mysteriously sticky—then pulled the boys onto his lap, holding them both so he could listen to their antics.

He couldn't remember when he'd seen the twins so animated or so happy. It was because of Natalie, he thought, touching her cheek gently again to awaken her.

"Nat?" He smiled, stroking her cheek as she mumbled something incoherent, then rolled over, her eyes fluttering.

"Jared?" A shadow crossed her features and she bolted upright, panic coursing through her. Jared had never been in her bedroom before. "What's wrong?"

He smiled, placing his hands on her shoulders to calm

her. "Nothing." Unable to resist, he gently massaged her tight muscles. "But it's almost eight, and I thought you might be getting hungry."

"Eight?" Disoriented, she clutched the sheet, tugging it up, aware that he was sitting on the edge of her bed, and she was dressed in a skimpy nightgown.

Blinking the sleep from her eyes, she glanced toward her bedroom window. Night had fallen, and the moon hung high and bright in the sky.

"Eight at night?" she asked with a frown, struggling to clear the grogginess from her head. Exhausted, she'd nodded off almost immediately after her bath.

He laughed, tenderly brushing her hair off her face. "Yes, at night. I understand you had quite a day." He'd never seen her look so vulnerable, or so provocative. Unintentionally, he thought. Unlike most women, who reveled in their beauty, Natalie seemed totally oblivious to it. In fact, she did nothing to enhance it and at times he wondered if she deliberately concealed it beneath those oversize shirts and leggings.

Provocative or not, he realized she was one of the most beautiful women he'd ever met—inside and out. And that, he realized, letting his gaze go over her face, was pretty important. He'd learned the hard way with Kathryn that a woman could be beautiful on the outside, but it was what was inside of her that really counted. Perhaps that's why he'd been so careful all these years.

A woman who loved herself too much had little room in her heart to love anyone else.

"It's still Halloween?" she said with a groan, making him laugh.

"It is. And you've missed dinner."

Her gaze flew to his as she pushed a tangle of hair out of her face. "What about you and the boys? Did you eat?"

"Tommy and I fed the boys, but I was kind of hoping…" Still caressing her shoulders, he found himself dealing with an unexpected bout of nerves.

He hadn't invited a woman out in so long he realized he was out of practice. "I was wondering if you'd like to go out for some dinner?" He wished his nerves weren't thrumming and he didn't feel like he was holding his breath, waiting for her response.

"Go out for dinner?" she repeated, as if he'd asked her to dance naked down Main Street.

He laughed again. "Yes, you know. You and me. A restaurant where someone else cooks and serves the food."

"No food fights?" she asked suspiciously.

"Nope." He shook his head, crossing his arms across his chest. She looked far too enticing and he feared if he didn't do something with his hands, they would end up around her, on her. And he'd been carefully keeping a leash on his emotions since the night he'd kissed her. He'd been so staggered, so stunned by the impact of that kiss that he knew just one was not going to be enough. He craved more.

And that frightened him enough to back off a bit. He'd been far too careful all these years to let hormones push him into something he'd regret.

Since she'd arrived, their relationship had slowly grown, until now they had what he considered a very solid friendship. Or at least that was the word his mind could accept.

He was at the point where he realized he could no longer deny his interest in Natalie—not just as the boys' nanny, but as something far more.

It frightened him, but he'd vowed to simply take things slow and not do anything foolish to jeopardize the friendship they'd developed, or her presence in his home and with his boys.

"Tonight, throwing food is *not* allowed," he said with a firm shake of his head.

"Thank goodness," she said with a pleasurable sigh that lifted her bare, slender shoulders.

It had been a long time since she'd had dinner alone with a man. And she suddenly found the thought of having dinner alone with Jared very appealing.

*Be careful,* she mentally warned herself, struggling to balance the pleasure she suddenly felt with the responsibility she carried. She couldn't afford to get involved with Jared. She couldn't afford to care about him.

*Too late,* her mind echoed. It was far too late, she realized, looking at his face, realizing somehow she'd grown to care about him, had become emotionally involved with him, his family, as well as his life.

Jared was unlike any man she'd ever met. Kind. Loving. Giving. Generous, and the most wonderful father she could ever have imagined or wanted for her children.

*But he isn't their father,* she had to remind herself once again, though the thought always brought on a mixture of pain and regret.

In the past few weeks, since Jared had kissed her, she'd found herself daydreaming, wondering what her life—and her children's lives—would have been like if Jared *had* been their father.

*Wonderful,* she realized sadly. Absolutely wonderful.

But wondering and wishing did not make it a reality, she reminded herself firmly.

Jared was *not* her boys' father.

But she was their mother.

And she couldn't ever forget the reality of the situation, not ever.

Soon, very soon, she was going to have to tell Jared the truth. Time was running out, she realized sadly, trying to bank the panic that rose at the thought of having to reveal to Jared exactly who she was and why she was there. She knew she couldn't contain or control her own feelings about Jared much longer. Or keep up this charade of who she was much longer.

He'd come to trust her and rely on her, and that's exactly what she'd wanted, intended. So why did it make her feel so miserably guilty?

Looking at him now, feeling the warmth of his body so close to hers, she clutched the sheet tighter, aware of his gaze going over her, setting off pulse points of tension within her and heating her skin until it felt as if his hands were touching her, not just his eyes.

Struggling to pick up the threads of the conversation and banish her wayward thoughts, Natalie licked her dry lips, aware that Jared's gaze followed the movement of her tongue, sending a wicked thrill dancing over her bare skin. He hadn't kissed her since that night in the yard, and she wasn't certain if she was relieved or remorseful.

"No feeding Ruth or Ditka under the table?" she asked.

"Not tonight, I'm afraid. They'll have to get their own dates."

*Date?* A flutter of nerves chilled her, and Natalie looked at him in surprise. She wasn't certain she wanted to consider this a date. It had too many connotations, too many implications she wasn't sure she could handle right now.

And it scared the daylights out of her. If she'd met Jared under different circumstances, she would have been thrilled about going on a date with a man like him.

But not like this.

The thought merely terrified her. A date would put their relationship on a whole different level, a personal level, one she knew she simply couldn't allow under the circumstances. She'd been desperately struggling to keep her feelings for Jared under tight control, knowing that any kind of personal relationship with him was an impossibility for more reasons than she could ever begin to name.

Even entertaining the idea of going on a date with him stirred up all kinds of images and feelings better left alone. No, she couldn't date him, couldn't go on a date with him, couldn't allow or encourage any personal feelings for him.

No matter what.

For his sake, she couldn't allow him to think she was available for a personal relationship with him. No matter how much she might want it. It was impossible under the circumstances, and would seem far more heinous and dishonest, when he learned the truth of their situation.

She knew she had to keep things on a professional basis. "No spilled milk or juice?" she asked, stalling nervously.

"Not unless I get clumsy." He touched her cheek, his gaze soft. "The boys were beat. I gave them their bath and tucked them in. Tommy's in for the evening, so he suggested we might want to get out for a little while." Jared's gaze drifted toward the window. "It's a beautiful night. There's a nip in the air, but it's almost the first of November so it's to be expected. But it's not so cool we can't enjoy the evening. I thought we might drive into town and have a nice, quiet dinner."

"So you're offering me a dinner I don't have to cook?"

"You got it." His gaze held hers. "What do you say?"

Feeling awkward, and more than tempted to just let things slide, she chose her words carefully, knowing she had to take a stand. "I'd say I'm starving, Jared," she said slowly, lifting her gaze to his and holding it in spite of the fact that it made her blood heat. "And your offer is very generous and much appreciated. But I think I'd feel better if we didn't call it a date."

Jared lifted one brow in surprise. but sensing something was going on that he didn't quite understand, he waited, trying not to feel stung.

"I work for you."

"Hmm, yes, I'm aware of that," he said with a smile, trying to ease whatever had caused her discomfort.

"And I just think it might be improper for me to date you."

"Improper," he repeated in surprise. "I see."

Wanting him to understand, Natalie touched his arm. "Jared, I'm sorry, but I just think we should keep things on a professional level. For the boys' sake." Another lie, she thought, watching his face. Would the lies she had to tell him ever end? "If something should happen..." Her voice trailed off and she searched for the right way to phrase this so as not to hurt or offend him, and yet not reveal the real reason she couldn't and wouldn't date him. "What if we find we dislike each other? Intensely?" His amused grin made her rush on. "Jared, I value my position here, and I don't want to do anything to jeopardize it."

"Nat." Sensing her distress, Jared lifted her chin, forcing her to look at him. "I'm sorry, it never occurred to me that you could interpret my asking you to dinner as improper." Still holding her gaze, he hesitated. "I hope you realize that nothing—nothing could jeopardize your position here. I told you, you're welcome to stay as long as you like. It's your choice. The boys and I..." He smiled, letting his voice trail off. "Well, let's just say we'd like you to stay forever, but—" He held up his hand to stop her protest "—I understand perfectly, and I'm glad that your position here is so important to you."

He admired her sense of honor and obligation, as well as her sense of propriety. It was touchingly old-fashioned, and nothing could have impressed him more. "So rather than call this a date, why don't we just say it's a grateful employer buying a very dedicated employee a much-deserved dinner out?"

She laughed, glad he'd taken it so well. "That sounds wonderful." Her stomach grumbled, and she pressed her hand to it. "Besides, I'm starving."

"Good." He stood up, then glanced at the clock on the nightstand. "I still have to shower and change, so why don't we meet in the living room in, say, an hour?"

"Perfect." She needed some time to pull herself together as well.

"Oh, and Nat," he said as he headed toward the door, "we found the lizard."

"You did?" Thrilled, she swung her legs over the side of the bed.

"Yep." He paused, turning to her with a smile just as she stepped barefoot out of bed. "But tread lightly. Matilda's still on the loose." Natalie's screech sent him laughing all the way down the hall.

## Chapter Five

"**I** hope you like steak," Jared said, as he slipped the valet his keys and went around to help Natalie from the car.

"I love it," she admitted, accepting his hand and ignoring the spark of electricity that arced between them. "Besides, I'm starving, and right now I'm not too fussy," she admitted with a laugh, glancing up at the restaurant.

"It's not real fancy, but the steaks, which they specialize in, are fabulous." He opened the door and led her inside. The restaurant had wood-paneled walls and an oak plank floor covered in sawdust. Candlelight flickered, casting long, soft shadows. "This is about the best restaurant in downtown Saddle Falls, not counting the Saddle Falls Hotel dining room," he added with a smile, taking her hand and following the hostess to their table.

Jared pulled out Natalie's chair, caught a whiff of her perfume and inhaled deeply, savoring the potent scent. She was dressed a bit differently tonight. Instead of jeans or leggings and a T-shirt, she had on a white pantsuit that showed off her figure. The jacket was double-breasted, and she'd worn it with a lightweight, silky blouse that dipped low in front to reveal just enough cleavage to make his mouth water.

She had on slender high heels, which brought her just about eye level with him. Her mouth was tinted a deep pink, and slightly shiny, making him ache to taste her.

Clearing his throat, and his thoughts, Jared went around and took his own seat. Their table was in a small alcove near a window, providing a beautiful view of the evening sky.

A waiter bustled over, pouring water, lighting the candle on the table and handing them each a menu. Natalie laughed when she looked at the selections offered. "You weren't kidding." She glanced across the table at Jared. "There's only steak and potatoes on this menu!"

He frowned a bit, more nervous than he'd been in years. Perhaps because he'd never spent more than a few minutes alone with Natalie. Tonight they had the whole evening alone together. "Would you prefer to go somewhere else?"

"No. Not at all." Still smiling, she shook her head and reached across the table to touch his hand, aware that he was probably just as nervous as she was. "This is perfect. Absolutely perfect."

She glanced around. There was a small smattering of other guests—a few couples, one large family and a few lone individuals—but there was enough privacy so they could talk.

Sipping her water, she watched Jared, amazed at the transformation in him. He wasn't wearing a suit, but had on clean, pressed jeans that molded his powerful legs like a glove, and a white dress shirt with a gray, pullover cashmere sweater.

His hair was still damp from his shower, and he'd

shaved. It gave her a slightly heady feeling to know that he'd gone to so much trouble just for their "non-date," as she'd started to think of it, and she was grateful she'd worn something other than her usual leggings and T-shirt.

She'd chosen a white pantsuit, casual, lightweight and very comfortable, and she'd worn her hair down. There was no reason to put it up tonight, since she didn't have to worry about chasing the boys or getting it caught in anything.

"Are you ready to order?" The waiter hovered, pen in hand. After taking their dinner order, he returned with a bottle of wine and a large basket filled with warm, crusty bread. The yeasty aroma made Natalie's mouth water. Famished, she broke off a piece of bread while the wine was poured.

"So are you recovered from your day?" Jared asked with a smile, leaning back in his chair and sipping his wine.

"I don't know that I'll ever recover," she said with a laugh, setting her bread down. "I never realized how rambunctious all those boys could be."

Jared watched the candlelight play over her beautiful features. "I'll bet, but do you think it did the trick? Do you think it's going to help Timmy?"

Wanting to reassure him, she covered his hand with hers. "I think so, Jared. He seemed very relaxed and comfortable with the boys, quite a few of whom had been teasing him." She shrugged. "You know how little boys are—they can be cruel one minute and best friends the next." She glanced up, surprised to find Jared watching her intently. "I've been working with him after school to recognize his letters and print them correctly. He's doing much better, but if you don't mind, I'd like to make an appointment to get his eyes examined. The boys will be off almost three days for Thanksgiving, and I'd like to bring him into town to have it checked out.'' She shrugged. "The problem might be something as simple as his vision.''

Jared nodded thoughtfully, then a slow, sexy smile curved his mouth, making her wary. "What?'' she asked. "Why are you smiling like the cat who ate the canary?''

Shaking his head, he laughed, lifting her hand and giving it the barest hint of a kiss, sending a thrill racing over her. "Because you continually amaze me.''

"Amaze you?'' she repeated in surprise, aware that he had laced his fingers through hers and was holding her hand. And she was enjoying it. "Why on earth do I amaze you?''

"Because of your instincts with the boys. You are absolutely totally in tune with their needs—physical, mental, emotional.'' He hesitated, not certain he should put this into words. He glanced at her and realized he needed to. "I'll bet you were a terrific mother.''

She froze and her gaze darted to his. For a moment, she wasn't quite certain what to say, how to respond. She simply stared at him, then swallowed hard, glancing down at the white tablecloth. "I...I like to think I was,'' she said quietly, "but most mothers are pretty intuitive about their children.''

"Kathryn wasn't,'' he said flatly, surprising her.

She glanced up at him. "I'm sorry.'' Not certain what else to say, Natalie sipped her wine.

Jared sighed. "Don't be sorry. I should have known, but I guess I wanted children so badly I didn't realize that she wasn't exactly mother material.'' He stared into his wineglass for a moment. "I met her while I was in Las Vegas for a cattle auction. It was one of those fluke meetings.'' He shrugged, but there was regret in his voice. "She was beautiful, I was smitten. My brothers tried to warn me that she was spoiled and selfish, but I wouldn't listen.'' He smiled wanly. "I wasn't exactly thinking clearly. We were married almost immediately."

"What did Tommy say?" she asked, watching him. She knew how important Tommy was to him. To all the Ryans, from the stories she'd heard.

"Tommy…" Jared blew out a breath, then dragged a hand through his hair. "At first, 'congratulations.' But Tommy's a big believer in family. You simply accept someone if they're part of the family, no questions asked."

She thought about the way Tommy had accepted her, and smiled. "That sounds like him."

"Anyway, Kathryn knew I wanted children, and we tried for several years. Finally, we talked about adoption. She didn't want to adopt," he said quietly. "She wanted to just give up the idea of a family, but I couldn't. I simply couldn't." He looked at Natalie, pain shadowed in his eyes. "Family is everything to me. To all us Ryans. The thought of being married and not having children was not something that ever occurred to me. Kathryn knew how I felt before we got married." He glanced around the room, then brought his gaze back to Natalie's. "Her father was some hotshot attorney in Vegas. He knew that we'd discussed adoption. I'd actually gone to him out of desperation to see if he could talk to Kathryn, to convince her to consider it. Well, he occasionally handled private adoptions, and had called because he was handling the adoption of twin toddlers—"

"Timmy and Terry?" she asked, praying her voice didn't betray the fear and anxiety coursing through her. Kathryn's father had placed her sons for adoption. It was difficult not to feel angry and resentful.

But she realized quickly she also should be grateful they had ended up with someone like Jared Ryan.

"Yeah." He took a sip of his wine. It suddenly tasted

bitter. "I said yes immediately. In fact, I went to get the boys myself."

"Your wife didn't go with you?" she asked, stunned.

"No, she was off skiing in Tahoe." The derision in his voice was hard to miss. "I had to make a quick decision, and I thought I'd made the right one. I thought she was comfortable with the idea of adoption."

"But she wasn't?" Natalie prompted.

He shook his head. "No. If anything, she was disappointed, because she wasn't anxious to be tied down." He smiled wanly. "If you think the boys are a handful now, you should have seen them at age two." He paused, lost in memories.

Natalie closed her eyes, envisioning the boys as they had been at two, the last time she'd seen them. She felt her heart crack a little. She'd had no idea then that it would be the last time she'd see them in over three years.

She and a neighbor had formed a play group. Since they both had two children, boys about the same age, each week one of them took all four boys for the afternoon, giving the other mother several hours free. Her neighbor, Jill, had the boys on the afternoon they'd disappeared. She'd taken them to the park. One of her own children had fallen, and while she was tending to him, the twins had simply vanished.

Raymond had no doubt been watching her, waiting for the right opportunity to snatch the boys. He knew about the play group, knew that all he had to do was wait for Jill to be distracted for a moment. And then he'd taken them. He'd called Natalie later that evening with his warning, telling her not to try to find the boys or they'd pay.

At the memory, Natalie's throat burned with unshed tears, and she had to take several deep, long breaths before she was certain she could contain her emotions and her tears.

"Kathryn simply freaked," Jared was saying. "She had absolutely no interest in the boys. Tommy and I took care of them. They were scared and a little traumatized. Their mother had apparently passed away, and they'd cried for weeks for her. Timmy couldn't sleep and had nightmares. He'd wake up three or four times during the night, crying for his mother." Saddened, Jared shook his head. "I'd walk the floor with him for hours, trying to soothe him. He was so scared his whole body would shake." Shaking his head, Jared blew out a breath. "Kathryn slept right through it, but it nearly broke my heart."

"The poor thing." Natalie's voice was a choked whisper and tears filled her eyes. The image of her son, her precious baby, being scared, having nightmares and crying out for her filled her with an unbearable sadness that was almost impossible to contain. Silently, she cursed Raymond again for doing this to her and her sons.

Jared squeezed her hand in comfort. "Within six months, Kathryn took off."

"You mean she just left?" Now that she knew them so well, Natalie was even more horrified that the woman could just walk away from Jared and Tommy, not to mention the boys.

"Well, she didn't just leave." Jared's smile was bitter. "She took a good chunk of my money with her. It was the only way I could get her to give up any claim to the boys."

Natalie had to swallow hard around the lump in her throat. "You mean you bought the boys from her?"

His startled gaze jumped to hers. "Well, I don't know that I'd go so far as to say that, Nat—"

"I'm sorry." Realizing how harsh her words had sounded, Natalie gave his hand a squeeze. "I didn't quite mean it that way, Jared."

He shrugged. "I wanted the boys, and I wanted to be

certain I never had to worry about her ever trying to claim them.''

Natalie frowned. ''But I don't understand. I thought you said she had no interest in them.''

''She didn't, but she did have a keen interest in my money.'' His face grew grim. ''She knew how much the boys meant to me.'' He shrugged again. ''Kathryn was not stupid. She knew I'd do anything to keep the boys safe and protect them.''

''So you paid her off?'' Natalie asked quietly, and he nodded.

''In a manner of speaking.'' He leaned forward. ''I'm not particularly proud of my behavior, Natalie, but you have to understand. Those boys mean the world to me. I'd do anything—*anything*—to protect them and keep them safe.'' There was a fierceness in his voice, a protectiveness that frightened her, for she had no doubt he meant it. ''It was only money.'' He shrugged. ''It meant nothing, not compared to the boys.'' He thought of his brother Jesse. The Ryan family would have given up their entire fortune to get him back, and wouldn't have thought twice about it. ''Can you understand that?''

Natalie felt a chill race over her and was grateful she had a moment to compose herself when the waiter approached with their entrees. ''Of course,'' she said quietly. ''It's perfectly understandable.'' Trembling now, she took another sip of her wine then picked up her fork, merely toying with her food. ''Have you ever heard from her? I mean, has Kathryn ever contacted you about the boys?''

He nodded. ''She calls about once a year to check in for whatever reason. Who knows what's going on in that head of hers? I just heard from her a few weeks ago. Guess she had a flash of guilty conscience. She called to see how the boys were doing, or so she says. Personally, I think she was running low on money and was going to hit me up. Her father passed away not too long ago, and from what I understand he died broke." Jared shrugged. "So I'm sure she thought she could come back to the Ryan money well again. But I didn't give her a chance. I made sure our call was brief."

Natalie's gaze searched his. "And what did you tell her?" Her fears for her sons were now doubled, knowing Jared's ex-wife might use them as a bartering tool.

He smiled, lifted her hand and kissed it gently again. "It gave me great pleasure to tell her we were doing absolutely wonderfully. That the boys had a brand-new, wonderful nanny and were thriving."

Natalie watched him carefully. "And what did she say?"

"Nothing. I guess I sort of took the wind out of her sails. She said she just wanted to check how things were."

"Do you believe her?"

He shrugged. "Doesn't matter whether I believe her or not." He cut into his steak. "It doesn't matter what she does as long as she stays away from the boys."

By the time their coffee was served, Natalie was almost certain she had her emotions and her nerves under control. Talk had turned from Jared's ex-wife Kathryn to the boys' antics the past few weeks, bringing some much needed relief to her jangling nerves.

Discussing the boys' recent adventures was a subject she felt safe talking about.

"It's hard to believe Thanksgiving is only a few weeks away," Jared said, slowly stirring sugar into his coffee.

"I know. This fall seems to have flown by." Smiling, she poured cream into her own, then took a sip, sighing in pleasure at the flavor.

"Will you be needing some time off to spend the holiday

with your family? Jake and Rebecca will be home, and I'm sure they'd be glad to pitch in and help with the boys."

Natalie glanced across the table at him, not certain how to answer.

Jared smiled at her, oblivious to her sudden discomfort. "Do you realize, Natalie, that even after all this time I don't know if you have parents, brothers, sisters?"

She glanced up, then away. "My mom died when I was six. My father raised me and my brother." She forced herself to look at him. "My brother was killed in a car accident when he was seventeen." She took a sip of her coffee, smiling wanly, the pain still strong after all these years. "It was devastating to lose him."

Cocking his head, Jared studied her. "Were you close?" he asked quietly.

She nodded. "Very. We were only two years apart, and after my mom died, we were sort of comrades-in-arms." She lifted her head to smile. "Then, just about two and a half years ago, my father passed away from a heart attack." A heart attack caused by the stress of Raymond's actions. Her nerves began to thrum and she shrugged. "So that's it. It's just me." Her throat was so dry, she took another sip of her wine, then reached for her water, preferring something cool to soothe her throat. "So no, I won't be needing time off to spend with family."

"I'm sorry, Nat." Smiling gently, Jared reached across the table and took her hand in his. "It must have been very difficult to have lost so many people you loved."

Something in his tone of voice caused her to look at him curiously. Tilting her head, she studied him over the rim of her cup. "You sound like you have some experience with loss?" Even in the candlelight, she could see that he paled, and it startled her. "Jared?" She touched his arm, alarmed. "I'm sorry, I didn't mean to pry." Her voice was tinged with regret.

"No. No." He blew out another breath and tried to smile, but simply couldn't manage it. "You're not prying." He stared into his coffee cup for a long, silent moment. "I have three brothers, Nat."

"I'm sorry, I don't understand. I thought Jake and Josh were your only brothers," she said, knowing she couldn't let on that she knew all about his family from the articles she'd read before she'd arrived.

"No." His voice was a low, hushed whisper. "There was Jesse as well."

The pain in his voice was so strong it was like a living thing, making his words vibrate with anguish. Her own heart began to ache for him. This was obviously something very, very painful to him, and she hated to see Jared look so tormented.

"Jesse?" she prompted softly, and Jared nodded.

"He was the youngest of the four of us." Jared lifted his cup, took a sip of coffee, then set it down again before raising his gaze to hers. "When Jesse was just about five, he was…he…disappeared." Jared's voice had gone flat, cold, emotionless. Natalie knew from experience what that was like—the supreme control it took to block the pain, to block the heartache, while inside you were devoid of life, an empty shell.

"Jared!" Horrified, she took his hand in hers, wanting to offer comfort, wanting to ease the tortured look on his face, in his eyes. "What do you mean, he disappeared? Five-year-old boys just don't disappear." How well she knew! she thought, her heart aching for Jared and his family.

He blew out a long breath, clutching her hand tightly in

his. "Jake, Josh and I went to a sleepover at a neighbor's. It was a last blowout before school started."

"Jesse didn't go?"

He shook his head. "No. He was only five. My mother thought he was too young to go on an overnight, especially since she and my dad were going out."

"What happened?"

"Our nanny came over to sit with Jesse." Jared glanced up at her and Natalie wanted to weep at the look on his face. "She left the house, leaving Jesse asleep and alone. When she returned, the front door was open and Jesse was gone." Jared dragged a trembling hand through his hair. He never spoke about Jesse with anyone. Couldn't even remember the last time he'd told anyone about his brother. Or the loss he'd felt all these years. "We...we never saw him again. Never found out what happened to him. He was just...lost." He glanced up at her. "We spent years looking for him, chasing false leads, paying informants, hiring private detectives."

"What about the nanny? Surely she must have known something?"

Jared shook his head. "No. They suspected she was involved and even questioned her, but they didn't have enough evidence to hold or charge her with anything, and she never changed her story that Jesse was fine and sleeping in his room when she last saw him. That she fell asleep on the couch watching TV, and when she woke up the front door was wide open and Jesse was gone." Jared dragged a hand through his hair. "Believe it or not, Rebecca, my brother Jake's wife, is the daughter of our nanny." He held up his hand. "Her mother recently passed away. Rebecca came back to Saddle Falls to bury her and to find out exactly what part her mother had played in Jesse's disappearance."

"And did she?" Natalie asked gently.

He shook his head. "Yes. During her investigation, she and Jake fell in love and married. That's why Jake and Rebecca are still traveling, following up more leads they received on Jesse's whereabouts."

Natalie's heart leaped. "Do you think they might be able to find him?" She knew from experience how difficult it was to find a child who had disappeared, knew from experience how many false leads and blind alleys you had to drive through to find one small kernel of information that might help you.

He shook his head. "I don't know." His smile was wan. "After all this time, I'm about ready to give up hope." His gaze met hers. "It's been so long, Nat. So very, very long."

She squeezed his hand. "Jared, don't ever give up hope, no matter how long it is, no matter how long it takes. All you need is one good lead, one positive clue, and that might be what leads you to him." The fervor in her own voice rang in her ears, and Natalie realized she was speaking about her own experience finding the boys. It scared her for a moment, knowing she'd allowed her own personal situation and emotions to come so close to the surface.

"I'm trying, Nat. But it's hard not to give up." Jared shook his head. "Jesse's disappearance almost killed my mother. I don't think she ever got over it."

"I don't think a mother ever gets over such a loss," Natalie said carefully. Hands shaking, she sipped the last of her coffee. "It torments you every moment of every day, wondering what happened to your child. If he's hurt, crying, safe. Every child you see, you search his face, hoping it's yours. But it never is," she murmured. "And at night, you see them, and invariably they're crying for you, but you can't reach them, can't find them." With a frightened shudder, she shook the image away, an image that she herself had lived with for almost three years. "They're simply...lost to you."

"I don't think my mother ever stopped blaming herself," Jared admitted.

"That's only natural, Jared." Natalie had to remind herself to breathe, not certain if she was talking about herself and her situation, or Jared's. "Mothers always feel responsible for what happens to their kids—good or bad—and for some reason we feel like we're omnipotent, able to protect our kids from any harm." She shrugged. "It goes with the territory. But one thing I've learned is that mothers are only human, too. We do the best we can and simply pray for the rest. It's all we can do."

"I know. But my mom took it so hard." He shook his head. "My parents were killed in a freak plane crash coming home from a business trip. It saddens me to think my mother died never knowing what happened to her youngest son." He took a deep breath. "I know her last thoughts were of Jesse." His voice was a husky whisper that caused Natalie's throat to close.

"Oh, Jared." Tears came, faster, harder, and slipped unheeded down Natalie's face. "I'm so sorry. So very, very sorry." She clung to his hand, then lifted it to her own lips, kissing it in comfort, the way he had done to hers during dinner. She wanted so much to hold and comfort him, to ease some of the pain he was feeling, the pain she had felt all these years because of the loss of her own children.

"Can we get out of here?" he asked abruptly, and she nodded. Jared stood, came around to pull out her chair, tossed some bills on the table, then took her hand, guiding her toward the exit.

The moment the door closed behind them, he stepped into a small alcove next to the entrance and dragged her to him, wrapping his arms around her, needing, wanting to hold her. Standing there in the darkness, where no one could see them, it was as if they were all alone in the world.

"Jared." Emotions high, Natalie clung to him, ran her fingers around the back of his head, pressed kisses to his cheeks, his jaw, his temple, wanting only to ease the pain and heartache she'd seen reflected in his eyes. "I'm so sorry," she murmured, her voice choked with tears. "So very sorry."

She knew exactly the kind of pain he was going through. Knew, too, how not knowing what had happened to someone you loved ate a hole in your heart—a wound that seemed to grow and fester with each passing hour and day.

"I'm sorry, too, Nat," he said quietly, drawing back and feeling a bit embarrassed by his display of emotions. "I don't usually talk about Jesse with anyone."

She searched his gaze, saw the depth of emotion and felt her heart ache. "Then I'm glad you talked about him with me."

He laid a hand to her cheek, let his fingers stroke and caress the silk of her skin. "I certainly didn't intend to tell you," he said, still struggling to understand why he had. "I guess I've just come to trust you, and not just with the boys." He brushed his lips against her forehead, pulling her close and into his arms again, wanting to hold her, to feel her body near his, warming him. "I haven't trusted anyone but family for a long, long time." Gently, he pushed her hair off her face, his gaze caressing her. "Being able to talk to you, to tell you things, to share things with you…" He hesitated, pressed his lips to her temple. "I can't tell you how much that means to me, Nat." He drew back, looked down at her. "Or how much you mean to me," he added quietly, lowering his mouth to hers.

"Oh, Jared." Natalie clung to him, lifting her mouth for his kiss, clutching the back of his sweater with her hands, pressing herself against him. She felt as if she were drowning, and he was the only lifeboat in sight. The touch of his lips was like a soothing balm that miraculously seemed to ease the pain and hurt that she had lived with so long.

"Natalie." Her name was a plea wrenched from his lips, filled with emotion, filled with such need she wanted to weep.

Jared Ryan trusted her.

And she was going to deceive him.

# Chapter Six

The following evening as Jared tucked the boys into bed, he had to laugh at their shenanigans. "Come on, Dad, just one more, please?" Snuggling deeper beneath the covers, Terry stifled a huge yawn.

"Yeah, please, Dad?" Timmy's voice from the adjacent twin bed was foggy with sleep as well.

"We like when you tell us stories 'bout when you and Uncle Jake and Josh were little."

"That's only because it gives you ideas," Jared said with a chuckle, ruffling Terry's hair.

"Nah," the boy said, using a fist to rub his eyes as he glanced up at his father, who was sitting on the edge of the small bed. "We got lots of ideas of our own."

Jared chuckled again. It was a nightly con. He always tucked the boys into bed and told them a story. The boys particularly enjoyed the stories he told about the trouble he and his brothers used to get into. Every night the twins tried to finagle an extra few minutes by pleading for another story.

Glancing at his sons, Jared found his heart filled with love. He really didn't mind, because it gave him some quiet, private time with the boys, time to simply enjoy them. A rarity in his very busy day. But this time every night was sacred.

He was always tired—exhausted, usually—but it was a satisfying feeling. His workday was finally done, all the chores behind him except for the never-ending paperwork, and he had nothing on his mind but spending time with the boys. Time he cherished.

He ruffled Terry's hair. "Well, as your dad, I can vouch for the fact that you've got enough ideas of your own. But it's a school night, sport, and you need your sleep."

Terry scowled. "No it's not, Dad. We don't got school tomorrow cuz of Thanksgiving."

Jared's brows rose suspiciously. "Thanksgiving isn't until Thursday."

"Yeah, Dad, but tomorrow *is* Thursday. Uncle Jake's coming home and we're gonna be in the Thanksgiving pageant and parade, remember?"

Jared frowned. Was it Thanksgiving already? He'd been so busy on the ranch getting ready for winter, and so preoccupied—no, so *content,* he mentally corrected—that the time had flown by. He remembered the day less than a month ago when he'd come in dead tired and found the boys nearly bouncing out of their shoes with excitement about having been chosen to be in the Saddle Falls Thanksgiving parade. Natalie had spent the last few weeks working late into the night sewing their Pilgrim costumes.

"So we don't gotta go to school until Monday," Timmy informed him, rubbing his eyes with his fists. "So come on, Dad, just one more story? Please?"

"Well, don't you have to be wide awake for the Thanksgiving parade tomorrow?" he asked with a lift of his brow.

"Yeah, but we don't got to get up too early."

Jared grinned. "Tomorrow, sport. I promise to tell you two stories tomorrow. And since you don't have to go to school on Thursday—'

"Turkey day, yeah!" Terry rubbed his stomach in anticipation.

"Yeah, turkey day, sport, I'll let you stay up an extra hour and watch TV."

"Great!" Delighted, Terry rolled over, tucking his fists under his pillow, a sure sign he was sleepy. "Dad?"

"Yes, Son? "

"Is Natalie gonna leave?"

"Why on earth would you think Natalie was going to leave?" he asked his son.

It took some effort, but Terry managed a shrug. "Dunno." He yawned, closing his eyes and snuggling deeper beneath the covers. "Because our mom left, and then all the other nannies left." He shrugged again. "So is she gonna leave, too?"

Jared brushed a hand over the little boy's head, feeling a deep, aching sadness in his heart. No wonder the twins expected every female to leave them. First their mom had died, then Kathryn had abandoned them, followed by a parade of nannies who'd come and gone. It pained him to know his sons had been hurt, at such a young age.

"No, Son," he said gently. "I don't think Natalie's going to leave."

"Could you ask her, Dad?" Terry shifted closer, snuggling against his father. "Cuz Christmas is coming soon and she promised to help make us new stockings for Santa."

"Yeah, Dad." Timmy piped up. "And she said we could even help decorate the tree now cuz we're big."

His heart filled with love, Jared bent to tuck the covers

over Terry and kiss his forehead. "Well then, if she promised to help you make new stockings, and to let you help decorate the tree, then I guess that means she's not planning on leaving."

"Think so?" Terry muttered sleepily.

"Yep. I think so." Jared turned to tuck Timmy in and give him a kiss.

"But could you still ask her, Dad? Please?" Timmy, always the worrier, pressed.

Jared smiled, running a hand over the boy's head. "Sure, Son. I'll ask her." He kissed him again. "I promise. Get some sleep now."

Rising, Jared glanced at the large Mickey Mouse clock on the nightstand. It had large numbers that glowed in the dark and served as a night-light. Natalie had bought it for the boys that first week, after she'd learned they were afraid of the dark. Other nannies had been critical of him for allowing the boys to have a night-light, but Natalie had merely accepted it and done what was necessary to make the boys comfortable.

He smiled, remembering her telling him that if the twins still needed a night-light when they got married, well then, maybe that would be the time to worry. But until then, it was perfectly normal and natural.

Jared flipped off the overhead light, then gazed at his sons for a long moment, his troubled thoughts on their question as he turned and headed out the door and down the long hall toward the kitchen.

"Are the boys asleep?" Natalie asked, glancing up from the counter she was wiping down when Jared walked into the kitchen.

"Out like two little headlights," he said, letting his gaze take her in. The kitchen window was open, allowing a crisp fall breeze to blow in, ruffling the white curtains at the window and gently stirring her hair, which she'd absently tucked behind her ears as she worked.

"Would you like some coffee?" Natalie asked as Jared headed toward the stove. "It's fresh and still hot, I think." With a smile, she laid down her dishcloth and reached for the pot. Jared reached for it at the same time and their fingers brushed, his covering hers.

Both of them froze for a moment.

Natalie slowly lifted her gaze to his, surprised to find him studying her curiously, those beautiful blue eyes clouded with an emotion she couldn't read.

Contact with him, even the slightest brush of their fingers always triggered something in her, something foreign and just a bit frightening. There was something powerful in Jared's touch, something that made her heart ache and her soul yearn.

No matter how she tried to deny it, her feelings didn't lie.

With a confidence that belied the tension storming within her, Natalie held his gaze. Heat streaking through her tense body from his casual touch, she tried to ignore the wild pounding of her pulse, her heart.

"Sorry." Forcing a bright smile, she relinquished the pot handle to him. Ever since Halloween night, when they'd gone to dinner and confided so much in each other—and Jared had kissed her in a way that left her heart and her head spinning—she'd tried hard to ignore the feelings that coursed through her every time he came near. Tried to ignore the feelings she could no longer deny.

In spite of everything, she was falling in love with Jared Ryan.

And she knew such a thing could have disastrous consequences.

But she was powerless to stop it, and at a loss as to what to do about it. She enjoyed the time they spent together. Every evening now, when Jared came in, they would have dinner with the kids. Then she cleaned up the kitchen and make lunches for the next day while Jared gave the boys their baths and tucked them in.

Just like a real family.

There was no way she could deny that she was enjoy-ing—relishing—the feeling of normalcy being here had given her. For the first time since the twins had been born, she felt as if she was giving them a normal family life. For the first time she felt content, at peace.

And she knew Jared was the cause of those feelings.

Tonight, she'd been lollygagging, happily daydreaming about Thanksgiving while making preparations for the big dinner she was cooking, and finishing up some last-minute details on the boys' costumes for the parade tomorrow. As a result, she hadn't quite finished cleaning up the kitchen when Jared came in.

A little off balance since she'd realized the depth of her feelings for him, Natalie picked up her dishrag and contin-ued wiping down the counter, forcing her smile to remain in place. She didn't want to reveal how she felt; it simply wouldn't be fair to either of them. If Jared ever learned the truth, there was no way they could have a future together, and she'd be foolish to believe otherwise.

"Did Timmy tell you he got an A on his spelling quiz today?" she asked brightly, glancing up at Jared, surprised to find he was still standing there, staring at her.

"No, he didn't." He smiled, reached out to brush a stray strand of hair behind her ear, letting his fingers linger for a moment. It was the first time he'd touched her all day, and he found he'd been looking forward to it. "That's ter-rific. I guess he's learning his letters better?"

She nodded, trying not to shiver from his touch. "Definitely. I'm very pleased with his progress. And the ophthalmologist today confirmed that Timmy's vision is perfect."

"You've worked very hard with him, Nat, I know that. Tommy tells me you've spent at least an hour every day painstakingly printing letters and numbers with Timmy, making a game out of it so it doesn't seem boring or monotonous to him."

She shrugged, uncomfortable with the praise, since it wasn't anything special, nothing any other mother wouldn't do with a child who was struggling in school.

"It's my job, Jared," she said softly.

"Yes," he said carefully. "It is. But you've gone way beyond the call of duty with your devotion and care of the boys."

"I love them," she said simply, no longer afraid for him to see the intense emotion she had for the boys. "They're truly wonderful kids."

"They love you, too," he said softly. She looked so perfect standing there in the kitchen, apron around her waist, dishrag in her hand, cleaning up just like any other wife or mother would after dinner.

Lost in his own thoughts, he continued to study her, still thinking about Terry's question about her leaving.

He simply couldn't bear the thought of her not being in their life.

"Jared?" She searched his face, saw something that made her stomach quiver. "What?" Instinctively, Natalie dropped the dishcloth and took a step closer, tension coursing through her. "Jared, what is it? Is something wrong?" Absently, she laid a hand on his bare arm, ignoring the warmth of his skin, the muscled strength beneath. "Are the boys all right?"

"The boys are fine, Natalie," he said softly, reaching out to stroke a finger down her cheek. He'd waited all day to see her, to touch her, and now that she was here, right in front of him, he simply couldn't resist.

She was standing so close to him now that every breath he took was filled with her fabulously feminine scent. It was incredibly intoxicating and made him want to draw her close and bury his face in her hair, the long, slender column of her neck.

"That's not the look of 'the boys are fine,'" she said skeptically, making him grin.

"Natalie," he began slowly, not certain how to phrase this. He was still reeling from the realization of how he felt about her. He had no idea how she might react if she knew, and he didn't want to do anything to make her uncomfortable around him. "The boys are very concerned about something. And they wanted me to talk to you about it."

"What?" Her gaze searched his. "What is it? Have I done something to upset them?" Her heart was hammering and her hand unconsciously tightened on his arm.

"No," he said with a gentle smile, taking her hand in his and holding it, relishing the soft silkiness, needing to have some physical connection to her. "It's nothing like that."

Relieved, she nodded. "Then what is it, Jared?" She clung tighter to his hand, as if bracing herself for a blow. "Please, just tell me. You can tell me anything."

His smile was slow and heartbreakingly sweet. "I know that, Nat," he said quietly, thinking about the night he'd told her about Kathryn and Jesse. Afterward, he'd lay in bed wondering why on earth he'd told her. Because he felt so comfortable with her, he realized now. Because he trusted her. Because he wanted her to be part of his life—his heart.

"The boys are concerned..." His voice trailed off and he looked helplessly at her. "The boys are worried that you're going to leave."

"Leave?" Caught off balance, Natalie merely stared at him, then shook her head. "I don't understand, Jared. Why on earth would they think I was leaving?"

"Why *wouldn't* they think you were leaving?" He smiled that slow, lazy smile that was somehow heartbreakingly sad. "In their experience, that's what women do." He shrugged. "They leave. First their mother, then Kathryn, then every other nanny—woman—who's been in their life."

"And so they think I'm going to leave them, too?" Stung, Natalie reeled for a moment, then quickly righted herself. She'd forgotten she could still be hurt, forgotten that she wasn't immune to pain, not when it came to the boys.

The moment the boys had disappeared, it was as if everything inside of her had frozen, shriveled and then died, to prevent her from feeling anything. Because if she *had* been able to feel, she would have to deal with the reality of what had happened, and she simply could not endure the pain of having *lost her children.*

She simply hadn't been able to cope with it, and so, as an act of self-preservation, she'd shut down her feelings, withdrawing into herself as a desperate form of protection.

Raymond had hurt her, yes, but by then her marriage was in serious trouble. She'd seen the real man beneath Raymond's charming facade, seen how she'd been deceived and, more importantly, used.

It had hurt, but she'd managed to cope with it, because by then her own feelings for him had long since withered and died, killed by his lies and cruelty.

But the feelings for her children were not something she

could simply ignore, and the pain of their loss had been so enormous she'd done the only thing she could to survive— she'd stopped allowing herself to feel.

But now, looking up at Jared, letting his words sink in, she realized it hurt deeply to know that her boys feared losing her, feared that she'd leave them. That they, too, had been hurt, hurt to the point where they *expected* to be left, to be abandoned.

They were far too young and innocent to have such terrible expectations, she realized sadly, and the mere thought almost broke her heart. She would never leave her children, would never have been separated from them by choice.

*But she'd had no choice.*

Because of it, her children had been victimized by a series of women who had not loved or understood them enough to stay with them, nurture them or care for them. And the knowledge hurt.

"Oh, Jared." Shaking her head, Natalie glanced down so he wouldn't see the sudden tears that filled her eyes. It had been a long time since she'd allowed herself the luxury of tears. Now she couldn't help it.

"I know," he said, understanding perfectly how she felt. He slipped his arms around her waist and gathered her close, wanting to comfort her, to ease her pain. Absently, he kissed the top of her head, savoring her wonderfully feminine scent.

She loved the boys completely and unconditionally, that was obvious—enough that their pain affected her. The fact moved him deeply.

"Don't cry," he said softly, touched beyond measure by the caring, the compassion this woman had for his boys. "I didn't tell you this to upset you." Gently, he rubbed her back, letting his fingers trail over the soft cotton of her shirt, feeling her warmth pressed against him, comforting him in return. "But so that, hopefully, we might be able to come up with a way to reassure them."

He rested his head against the top of her head, smiling because she'd stiffened when he'd pulled her into his arms, as if it still surprised her that he wanted to.

He had a feeling, judging from the look that came over her every time they touched, that she hadn't had much experience with men.

She looked almost surprised that there was this attraction between them—strong, vibrant, almost a living, breathing entity. He suspected that she didn't quite understand it or recognize it.

Unfortunately, he couldn't claim the same ignorance. He not only understood and recognized it, but was beginning to enjoy it, despite the fact that warning bells should have been going off in his head.

"Considering their history, I think the boys' expectations are perfectly understandable, don't you?" he asked quietly, drawing back to look at her. Using his thumb, he wiped away a tear.

"Absolutely," she admitted, feeling guilt crash over her like a tidal wave, engulfing her—guilt that she'd failed to protect her children from the pain of being hurt, of loss, of the fear of abandonment.

Her sons had been defenseless, at the mercy of strangers, and she hadn't been around to protect them or to do anything about it. Her fists clenched as the full impotency of the situation hit her once more.

From the moment the boys had been born, the moment she'd glanced down and seen their beautiful faces, something had erupted inside of her. It was a kind of fierce, loving protectiveness, the sort she'd never have believed possible if she hadn't actually experienced it herself.

From that moment on, she'd mistakenly believed she

could protect her children from any kind of pain, shield them from all of life's sorrows. She'd believed it simply because she loved her sons so fiercely she knew she'd do everything necessary to protect her boys and always keep them safe.

It had been a sad and bitter lesson to learn she couldn't. How could she have been so wrong?

She was their mother, and yet she'd failed to protect her boys, on so many levels that she wasn't certain they'd ever be able to forgive her.

Worse, she wasn't at all certain she'd ever be able to forgive herself for the untold damage that had been done to her children, damage she'd been helpless to prevent.

Resolutely, she blinked her tears away, then sniffed, tilting her head to look at Jared, forcing herself to hold his gaze. "But Jared, I have no intention of leaving the boys. I can honestly say the thought has never even crossed my mind." She hesitated, choosing her words very carefully, knowing she couldn't afford to say anything that might give herself and her real purpose away. "I like it here very much. You've made me feel more than welcome." Lowering her gaze, Natalie glanced at the buttons on Jared's work shirt, unable to continue looking directly at him because it made her pulse dance so wickedly. "You've all treated me almost like...family," she said softly, ignoring the bitter remorse that nibbled away at her for the deception she was playing on all of them.

"I'm glad," Jared said. Her words helped relieve some of the tension he'd felt, but there was something else in the depths of her eyes, something he couldn't identify. For some reason it sent off a different kind of warning bell in his head. She looked disturbingly wary and uncomfortable, and he didn't understand why. "Then you're happy here?"

Natalie had to swallow the lump in her throat. How could

she ever explain that during the past few months here—being with her children, with him, providing a stable, secure home for her boys—she'd been happier than she'd ever been in her life?

"Very," she said softly.

Relieved, Jared grinned. "Good. I want you to be happy, Nat."

The way he said it made her realize he was talking about more than just her position here. He was inferring something far more personal, and it made her tense. "Jared?"

Blinking, he glanced back down at her.

"What about you, Jared?" she asked quietly, fighting off the sudden need she felt to lay her head on his broad chest and just rest for a moment. It had been such a long, harrowing three years.

So long.

Now the strain of being around her boys and not being able to claim them yet was wearing on her. She wanted them to get to know her well enough so they wouldn't be afraid, so she wouldn't hurt them any further. But trying to keep up a facade in front of Jared, while worrying every moment that Raymond would find them, was taking its toll.

She was just so weary. It felt as if she hadn't had a moment of peace, or a moment to rest, since the boys had been snatched. So the thought of laying her weary head on Jared's chest and just holding him and being held of allowing herself to just let go and relax, to forget all the problems and issues she was facing, was unbearably tempting.

Jared had strong, broad shoulders a woman could lean on. But it was a temptation she couldn't give in to. She couldn't need him and she couldn't lean on him. She knew it, but somehow her heart didn't seem to be getting the message.

Natalie couldn't stop looking at him, wishing she could

read what was in the depths of his eyes. "What do you expect, Jared?" she asked softly, nestling closer to him.

He was quiet for a moment, simply studying her, losing himself in those gorgeous, suddenly sad eyes, that beautiful face.

"Never mind," she finally said with a weary sigh, pushing her hair off her face, not giving him a chance to answer. Perhaps she didn't really want to know, couldn't afford to know. "I can read it in your face. You expect the same thing from women, don't you?" The sadness in his eyes almost broke her heart. "You expect us all to cut and run, right?"

"I guess, Nat, our expectations are based on our personal history." He shrugged. "And my past tells me not to expect much from a woman."

"I can understand that," she said slowly, realizing he had every right to expect her to be like his ex-wife. Still, she didn't like being compared to a woman she clearly had nothing in common with. "But I think you should understand that I'm not your ex-wife, nor am I like any other woman you've ever met, or nanny you've ever hired. So please don't lump me in with any of them. I'm me. And I don't cut and run if the going gets tough. Not my style." Her chin lifted in determination. "I have no intention of ever leaving the boys, Jared." Her eyes flashed. "Not ever."

Her dander was up, her eyes flashing, her mouth slightly pursed. And it was, he thought, an absolutely beautiful mouth. Full. Lush. The kind of mouth made for the pleasure of kissing. Jared couldn't stop staring, wondering, wanting.

Needs rose to mock him, reminding him again that he was still a normal, healthy man, a man who'd deliberately cut himself off from women simply to protect himself. At the moment, looking at Natalie, he simply couldn't remember why he thought he needed protection.

"Natalie."

He said her name in a soft, sensual whisper, making every thought in her head scatter and her pulse leap.

Those eyes...Natalie thought hazily, mesmerized in spite of herself. She allowed him to draw her closer until their bodies were touching, brushing up against one another, her softness resting against his masculine hardness. The knowledge sent a sizzling wave of awareness over her entire body.

"W-what?" Swallowing became difficult when he slipped his free hand around her waist, the pressure of his fingers warming her, reminding her he was touching her.

Breathing had become difficult as well. As long as she looked at him, as long as he continued to look at her like that, she knew she was going to have difficulty. It was as if some unknown force field was surrounding them, tugging them closer and closer while blocking out everything else but the two of them.

"I don't want you to leave," he whispered, knowing she was too close, and his desire too out of control at the moment for him to think clearly. All he could do was feel— feel all the emotions, the desires he'd kept buried for so long.

Natalie had somehow stirred and awakened them, until now they were clamoring to be set free.

"Good," she whispered, unable to draw her gaze from his. She was usually a strong person, in control, but his touch, the way he was looking at her, had made her knees wobbly. He was still holding her hand, and she clutched it now, fearing that if she didn't, her knees might buckle.

She wasn't used to having a man look at her like Jared

did. Hungry eyes, she thought absently, watching him as if in a fog. The man had hungry, haunting eyes.

She knew he'd been hurt, and she hated it—hated it more because she was going to hurt him as well.

She didn't want to, she realized with a growing sense of sadness. She didn't want to be the cause of any more pain for him. He didn't deserve it.

"Natalie." He said her name again, a soft, gentle whisper, tightening his hand around her waist to draw her even closer.

Her eyes widened a fraction as she watched his head lower, his mouth come closer. Instinctively, she raised a hand to his chest to push him away, knowing she couldn't allow this to continue any further. She was getting in too deep, allowing her emotions to overrule her intellect.

She had to stop him.

Instead, she found her fingers clutching the soft cloth of his shirt as she clung to him, lips parted, eyes wary, waiting.

His mouth brushed over hers slowly, gently, as if testing the waters. Her fingers tightened on his shirt and she tilted her head back, knowing she was weakening, remembering the whirlwind he caused every time he touched her, kissed her. Her breath was unsteady, her knees shaking, her stomach rolling.

She couldn't allow this, couldn't let herself become any more emotionally involved with him.

She couldn't afford to care about him.

"Jared." His name was a whisper, part fearful, part pleading, and he answered by covering her mouth fully with his.

The touch of his lips on hers, the feel of him so close brought out a shuddering breath of surprise, delight and desire, silencing all the warnings.

There was an intensity about his kiss, a heightened intent that both frightened and excited her beyond reason.

She'd never been kissed like this, never felt as if the floor had suddenly slid out from beneath her, leaving her dangling in midair, breathless, holding on to him simply because there didn't seem to be anything else to hold on to.

She knew she should push him away, knew she couldn't—shouldn't—do this, but she couldn't seem to help herself. The touch of his mouth on hers, so gently so delicious, turned her world upside down.

A whimper came from deep in her throat as his lips, soft, pliant and so very, very gentle, caressed hers. Drawn in, seduced by a multitude of sensations that slammed into her with stunning clarity, she knew instinctively she'd never felt any of this before. Never experienced this kind of mind-blowing, lung-stealing desire.

A tremor of awareness, of need, rippled through her, and she shivered, kissing him back with the same intensity, knowing she could do no less. She clung to him, winding her arms around his neck, drawing him closer, lifting up on tiptoe to better accept the fullness of his mouth.

Her breasts ached, tingled as his arms tightened around her, pulling her against him until she could feel his heart beating along with hers, as if they'd simply become one.

Staggered, Jared found his mind splintering, found himself becoming little more than a mass of feelings. Logic, reason deserted him as need and desire swept everything else away.

He'd felt a sense of urgency when the fear of her leaving had surfaced, and he realized now just how much she'd come to mean to him. How much he needed her, when he thought he'd never allow himself to need anyone again, especially a woman.

All his feelings and emotions came pouring out the moment she lifted her lips to his. Never had one woman undermined him so. He was a man of control, lived his life by it and didn't really know any other way to be. But from the first time he'd touched Natalie, kissed her, her nearness had shattered his control, leaving him stunned.

His lungs hurt as his breath labored in and out; his loins ached with the need to make her his, to brand her with his body, his touch.

He couldn't remember ever wanting a woman this much, couldn't remember being so totally consumed with feelings that everything else faded into oblivion.

This felt so right, he thought hazily, unwilling to allow any of his nagging thoughts to gain hold. It felt absolutely, totally right.

The thought slammed into him, frightening him when he realized what he was doing, and what he had at stake.

He shouldn't have done this, shouldn't have allowed it to happen. Getting involved with Natalie could only complicate the situation, and could be just the impetus to make her leave.

He couldn't risk it.

It had just been too long, he told himself. He'd denied himself the simple pleasures of a woman's company for so long it was only natural that he would respond so strongly to her. That's all it was, he told himself, reluctantly drawing back from her. But he didn't believe it for a moment.

Shaken, he lifted his head, looked at her. Her lips were still slightly parted and looked far too enticing for his peace of mind. Her eyes were hazy with passion, her lids slightly lowered, giving her an incredibly sexy look that he knew would haunt his dreams.

She swayed a bit on her feet, and he lifted his hands to her slender shoulders to steady her, wanting nothing more than to pull her back into his arms again and kiss her until they were both breathless, senseless and sated.

The yearning that had sprung to life the moment he'd laid eyes on her hadn't diminished, it had grown in the ensuing months. Being around her every day, seeing her, enjoying her company, the way she treated the boys, had only made him want her more.

"Natalie…" He let his voice trailed off, not certain what to say. Not trusting the thoughts in his mind.

"What, Jared?" Her voice was whisper soft, seductive, and her hands still clung to him.

He swallowed, wishing he'd had more time to plan, to think this through. "I want you to think about something."

Confused, she nodded, wondering how he could expect her to think about anything when he'd just kissed her silly. "Okay."

He had to swallow again, since his throat had gone bone dry. "Natalie, up until now, we've had a very professional relationship." He hesitated, not certain how to put into words what he was feeling. "I want you to think about making our arrangement more personal."

"Personal?" Panic skittered up her spine as his meaning sunk in. She could feel her body begin to tremble, partially in fear, partially in remorse.

She knew what he was asking, and realized she wanted nothing more than to throw her arms around him and agree. But she knew she couldn't—wouldn't. She simply couldn't allow Jared to harbor the illusion that there could be anything personal between them. And it left her infinitely sad at the cruel twist of fate that had brought this wonderful man into her life. If circumstances were different… Her thoughts trailed off. Circumstances weren't different, she reminded herself firmly, and wishing they were wouldn't accomplish anything except to give them both false hope, something she simply couldn't do.

"Jared—"

Seeing the look in her eyes, Jared lifted a finger to her mouth. "No, don't answer me now. I said I wanted you to think about it. I know this is sudden and a bit unexpected, and because you work for me it can also be a bit complicated, but I think it's worth the risk, Nat. I want more than an employee-employer relationship. And I think you do, too. We both know that we have something very special and very precious between us." He took a breath. "I just want you to think about making this—what's between us— more personal. I want to see you—not just professionally. But I want us to get to know each other personally."

Words wouldn't come, but tears did. Tears of regret and remorse, because if the circumstances had been different, she would have been overjoyed at Jared's request.

Now it merely broke her heart.

Looking at Jared, seeing the hope in his eyes, she knew she had run out of time.

She was going to have to tell him the truth.

She had no choice.

Natalie squeezed her eyes shut and said a prayer for courage. She'd have to tell him, but not now, not tonight. It was late, he was tired and she still had things to do tonight to ready the boys' costumes for the parade tomorrow.

She'd tell him after Thanksgiving.

By then, hopefully, all the hubbub of the holiday would be over and things would go back to normal. She'd have some quiet time to try to explain the truth to him.

She simply couldn't do it now. She couldn't. She wanted just a few more days to enjoy him and the boys, and the wonderful life they had.

Two days, she thought, exhaling deeply, feeling as if she'd been given a slight reprieve. She would give herself two more days, and she intended to enjoy them. She wouldn't have Jared in her life in the future, but perhaps she'd have the memories of the next two days to keep her company. It would have to be enough.

"Nat?"

He was waiting for an answer. Licking her lips, Natalie stroked the back of his head, deliberately getting her emotions under control. "Yes, Jared, I'll think about it." She managed a smile. "I promise."

Relieved, he smiled back, then brushed his lips against her forehead. "Thanks." Their gazes held for another long moment. The evening breeze ruffled the kitchen curtains, tossed her hair a bit, surrounded them.

Jared's blood was still simmering, his heart slamming recklessly. He knew he had to return some semblance of normalcy to the situation.

"Natalie, about the boys..." His voice trailed off as she nodded.

"Do you want me to talk to them, Jared? To reassure them I'm not leaving?"

He shook his head. "Why don't we just wait until after Thanksgiving, after we've had a chance to talk?" His smile was slow and hopeful and almost broke her heart. "Maybe then we can talk to them together, and maybe we'll have something to tell them that will erase their fears."

Biting her lip in worry, she nodded. "That's fine. After Thanksgiving will be fine. "

He looked at her for another long moment, knowing that if he stayed here he'd just drag her into his arms and finish what he'd started, what his body was clamoring for him to do. "Well, it's late. I think I'll turn in."

She glanced around. "And I'd better finish cleaning up.

Morning will be here before I know it and I've still got a couple things to do on the boys' costumes.'' She smiled up at him, not really wanting him to go. She lifted a hand to his cheek. ''Thanks, Jared, for confiding in me about the boys. It meant a lot to me.''

''Well, making sure that they're comfortable and secure is of the utmost importance to me, and to you, I'm sure. I thought it was important that you know of their concerns.'' He drew her closer, then brushed his mouth tenderly, lightly against hers, not wanting to linger for fear of losing himself again. It took supreme effort to draw away from her rather than draw her to him. ''Well, I think I'll call it a night.'' He was having a hard time leaving, not wanting to break this unbelievable connection between them.

She nodded, releasing his hands, knowing if she didn't, he might not go. She might not let him. ''Good night, Jared,'' she said with a smile, turning back to the counter and picking up the rag she'd carelessly dropped just a few minutes ago.

He stood there awkwardly for a moment, shifting from foot to foot. ''Good night, Nat.'' Wanting to touch her once more, he gently ran a hand down the silky curtain of her hair.

''Sleep well, Jared.''

Deliberately, she kept her back to him until she was certain he was out of the room. She could hear his boots echoing down the long hallway, and let out a weary sigh.

Sagging against the counter, Natalie closed her eyes and concentrated on taking several long, deep breaths, wondering how on earth she was going to tell him the truth.

She hadn't counted on this complication with Jared, hadn't counted on falling in love with him.

But she had, and now there was simply no denying it. Not to herself, not to him.

And she had no idea how to tell him the truth.

Two days, she thought again, straightening and pushing her hair off her face.

She had two days to figure out a way to break Jared's heart.

# Chapter Seven

"Nat! Nat!" Terry raced in the front door, lower lip trembling, eyes swimming with tears. "My hat! I lost my Pilgrim hat." He bounced from foot to foot, his hands flailing helplessly. "I can't find it." Tears slipped down his cheeks, dripping off his chin. "I thought it was in the car, but it's not, and I can't be in the parade without a hat."

"Shh, baby, shh." Nat hurried to him, going down on her knees and enfolding him in a hug. He looked utterly adorable in his brown muslin pants and shirt with the large collar, big black buttons and shiny black belt. His dark hair was tousled even though she'd combed it less than fifteen minutes ago. "We'll find it, sweetheart. Don't cry." She pressed a kiss to his forehead, then wiped his tears with a tissue. "Now tell me, where did you see it last?"

Wiping his drippy nose with his arm, Terry sniffled, then hiccuped. "Dunno." He scratched his head. "I think Ditka and Ruth were playing with it while we was eating breakfast."

Natalie wanted to groan. She should have made an extra

hat just for the blasted dogs, she thought. One or the other of them had been trying to snatch the boys' hats since the day she'd started making them. Something about the large, pointed things apparently fascinated the two dumb mutts.

"Okay, honey, where were Ditka and Ruth playing with it last?"

Terry shifted from foot to foot, scowling as he thought. "When we was eating breakfast, I think they took it out of my bedroom, but Grandpop took it away from them and brought it back." He shrugged his slender shoulders. "And then I thought I took it to the car, but it's not there." His eyes swam with tears again. "And now I'm not gonna be in the parade," he blubbered, throwing himself against her and wrapping his skinny arms around her neck.

"Shh, baby, don't cry." Hugging him, she patted his back. "You're going to be in the parade. We'll find your hat, I promise." Natalie glanced at her watch. They were due at the parade staging area in less than twenty minutes, and she still had to pack up the juice boxes and snacks she'd bought for the boys, since they wouldn't be having dinner until later in the afternoon. She'd put the turkey in the oven just a few moments ago and crossed it off her to-do list, but there was still a mountain of things to do—foods to prepare and a table to set.

Jared and Tommy had pitched in as much as possible, but they were basically useless in the kitchen. Besides, she was enjoying preparing this, the first holiday dinner she'd spent with family in many years.

While she was at the parade with Tommy and the boys, Jared was going to the airport to pick up his brother Jake.

Ignoring her own panic at all the tasks left undone, she drew another tissue out of her jeans pocket to wipe Terry's tears. "Now, tell you what." Smiling, she glanced around him out the open front door. "Is Timmy in the car?"

He nodded. "Grandpop's with him."

"Okay, you go on out to the car and ask Grandpop and Timmy to help you look out back, in the doghouse and your playhouse, to see if those fool dogs took it there, okay? And I'll search inside the house." She smiled encouragingly. "Okay?"

He nodded, wiping his eyes again. "Okay."

She held the tissue to his drippy nose. "Now blow." He did, thoroughly and noisily, making her laugh. "You sound like a goose, you silly goose." She tickled his belly until he giggled, tears forgotten. "Now go see if you can find your hat." She turned him around and gave him an affectionate pat on the behind. "I'll check around in here."

He raced toward the door, then skidded to a halt to turn back with a worried look.

"Nat?"

"Yes, honey?"

"You're not gonna be mad at the fool dogs, are you?" He looked so concerned, she laughed again.

"No, sweetheart. I'm not going to be mad at them."

"Cool." Grinning, he raced out the door.

With a sigh, Natalie stood, mentally organizing all the things she had to do in just a few moments. She went back into the kitchen and quickly pulled the snacks together, setting them on the table to pack. She was just reaching for the box of graham crackers in the pantry when the phone rang. Absently, she reached for the receiver, her gaze scanning the kitchen for Terry's hat, making a mental note to pull out the frozen topping from the freezer or they'd have no holiday dessert.

"Ryan residence," she said, juggling the phone with her shoulder while closing her fingers on the box of crackers.

"Hello, Natalie. It's been a long time."

Everything inside of her froze and the box of crackers slid from her fingers, bouncing to the floor.

"Raymond." Her voice was a hoarse, terrified whisper and her heart seemed to stop for a moment in sheer, unadulterated terror.

"You never did listen very well, now did you, Natalie?"

She squeezed her eyes shut, trying to stop the panic that slid over her like an insidious snake. Her gaze went to the front door and beyond, to where she knew the boys were.

*The boys!*

If Raymond knew where she was, then that meant *he knew where the boys were.*

Oh God!

Her fingers clutched the telephone receiver until her knuckles turned white.

"W-what do you want?" She closed her eyes, forcing herself to concentrate. She couldn't fall apart now; she had to find out what he wanted, and more importantly, how much he knew. Although her hands were shaking, she forced herself to calm down and take a deep breath.

"I thought you understood what I wanted, Natalie. But apparently I was wrong." There was a long pause that caused cold fear to trickle down her spine. "So tell me, how are *our* children?"

The tone of his voice, the mere fact that he'd even mentioned the boys, infuriated her, snuffing out some of the fear, replacing it with a white-hot fury.

"Listen to me, Raymond," she fairly hissed, her vision hazed by a protective maternal fury so strong it nearly overwhelmed her. "If you come near my boys again, if you ever try to contact them, if you ever do anything to hurt them, I swear I'll—"

"You'll what, Natalie?" He laughed, and the sound sent wicked shivers racing through her. He was mad, truly mad.

"You disobeyed me once, remember? You refused to ask your father to drop the charges against me, and do you remember what happened?"

Oh God! Feeling suddenly weak, she almost sank to her knees. She remembered all too well. *He'd stolen her children.* Her breath hitched, coming in short gasps as she tried to fill her aching lungs with air.

"I thought you'd be reasonable, use your influence with your father to get him to drop the charges against me, but you wouldn't, would you, Natalie? No, pure little Natalie couldn't lower herself to go to her father and ask him to do this one little thing for her—"

"You embezzled over two million dollars from my father," she yelled, tears clogging her throat.

"In retrospect, a mere pittance compared to the value of our children, don't you think?"

"They're not your children," she snapped fiercely, pressing a hand to her forehead. A deep, aching throb had started just above her eyes. "And I'm warning you, you'd better stay away from them, Raymond."

"Warning me?" He laughed again, the sound a bit more hysterical and desperate, terrifying her even more. "Natalie, you're in no position to be warning me about anything. Gotta go, Nat. I'll be seeing you. And the boys," he added in a hideous whisper just before the phone went dead.

Frozen in terror, Natalie stood there a moment, unable to move. What she'd feared for so long had now come true.

Oh God, what was she going to do?

Pressing her fists to her eyes, Natalie struggled to control her panic. She couldn't fall apart now; she simply couldn't. She had to *think!*

She had to protect the boys. This time she would take no chances, nor would she underestimate Raymond.

"Lassie, are you all right?" Tommy stood in the open

doorway, looking at her with a curiously concerned expression.

Struggling to contain her emotions, Natalie took a deep breath, hung up the phone and picked up the box of crackers she'd dropped. "I'm fine, Tommy," she said, turning to him and praying he wouldn't be able to see her fear. "Just dropped the crackers." She set them on the table with the rest of the snacks, her hands trembling.

With a slight frown, Tommy came to her, taking her hands in his. "Lass, what is it?" His gaze searched her face. "Whatever it is, we'll help, Natalie. You've only to tell us and we'll help."

His kind words were her undoing. "Tommy." Her voice trembled and the tears came, tears of fear, of terror. She wanted nothing more than to tell him the truth, to tell him about Raymond and the boys, and how frightened she was that he would do something to harm them, now that he'd found her and the boys again.

But she couldn't.

Couldn't tell him because it would break his heart to know that she'd knowingly and willingly deceived him and his family.

"There, there, lass, nothing can be that bad." Tommy gently took her in his arms, rocking her slowly. "Let it out and you'll feel better," he encouraged, patting her shoulder as she sobbed.

"Terry's hat is lost." It sounded silly and ridiculous, but it was all that came to mind. She couldn't tell Tommy the truth. Not now. Not like this.

"Yes, lass, I know. Terrible thing it is, but I've come in to tell you we found it. Ditka and Ruth were about to bury it in the backyard. Had the hole almost dug when we caught them in the act.'' He drew back, noting the absolute terror on her face, and knew that whatever had caused her tears, it wasn't a lost hat. "All's well now, Nat. Don't cry."

But she couldn't seem to stop. He continued to hold her, to rock her, and she allowed herself to lean on him and let go…just let go, letting the tears and her fears come pouring out.

"I miss my father," she said, her voice muffled by tears. It was so true. At this moment she wished her father were alive, wished she could lean on him, confide in him, knowing she wouldn't have to face Raymond or her fears alone. She'd never felt so alone in her life. Alone and terrified. "It's the holiday and—"

"Aye, so that's it, lassie." Tommy nodded, holding her gently. "Well, lass, it's understandable. But know that you have a family here, in us." He smiled, pulling a clean, pressed handkerchief out of his back pocket and handing it to her. "Know that the Ryans are your family now." He tilted her chin up. "You're one of us now, lass. Aye, perhaps not by birth, but by love.

"And know too, lass, that whatever it is that's troubling you, you're not alone. Aye, not alone at all. The Ryans will stand with you, no matter what the problem."

"Oh, Tommy," Natalie sobbed, not knowing what to do, what to say, how to even begin to explain the truth of who she was and why she was here.

Or that by coming here, she'd put the boys in danger.

She couldn't think of anything except that she had to protect the twins, keep them safe from Raymond and his insanity.

And she knew in her heart there was only one person who could help her do that: Jared.

\* \* \*

Natalie went through the day in a fog, doing all the things expected of her, but not really focused on anything except her own fears.

She was surprised to find that Jake, Jared's older brother, was a taller version of Jared. A little bit rougher, a little bit more cynical, but still almost a carbon copy. She liked him immediately.

His wife, Rebecca, whom she'd learned was an investigative reporter, and expecting her first child, gave her a moment of worry, fearing she might sense her distress in the way that women have. But Rebecca was genuinely nice and gracious, pitching in to help serve the meal, and Natalie took to her immediately.

Dear Tommy never took his eyes off of her, watching and worrying. She knew it, but couldn't seem to do anything to ease his concern, not when she had so much to worry about herself.

All through dinner, Natalie listened to the conversation with half an ear, trying to stay involved. But between watching the twins so they didn't turn dinner into a disaster, and her own concerns, she was not much of a participant.

As soon as dinner was completed, she cleaned up the boys and sent them to their room to play quietly until she could give them their baths and get them ready for bed. They were utterly exhausted from excitement and fatigue. The parade this morning had worn them out.

Once the boys were in their room, her concerns about not taking part in the conversation passed quickly when she realized that the after-dinner conversation revolved around Jake and Rebecca's trip to Texas, and possible clues leading to the discovery of what had happened to Jesse.

"So do you think this is just another wild-good chase?" Jared asked his brother over coffee as Natalie began clearing the table. "Or do you think it might be a solid lead?"

It had been too many years, with too many false leads, for him to get his hopes up yet.

Jared reached under the table for Rebecca's hand and held it tightly. "I'm not sure, bro. We've tracked down the woman who called me after Rebecca's story broke."

Rebecca's story about the Ryan family—including information about Jesse Ryan's disappearance twenty years ago, and the impact the Ryan family had had on the history of the Saddle Falls area—had run in the local paper a few months before. A picture of the entire Ryan clan had been included, which was how Harry Powers, the investigator Natalie had hired, had recognized the boys.

Rebecca's story had also sparked a lot of interest in Jesse Ryan's disappearance, and since its publication, calls and leads had been coming in. Rebecca and Jake had been personally checking out every single one.

"The lady who said she might have some information on Charles, the man you think was involved in Jesse's disappearance?" Jared asked now with a frown, sipping his coffee.

Jake nodded, glancing affectionately at his wife. "Yeah. Apparently her sister used to live in Saddle Falls, right about the time Jesse disappeared. Seems she was going out with a married man named Charlie, too."

"Think it's the same guy?" Jared glanced at Natalie, then smiled as his heart gave a pleasant bump. He was grateful she was here for this, grateful she'd had a chance to meet his brothers.

"Sure sounds like it," Jake admitted, glancing around the table at his family.

"Even if it is, where do we go from here?" Josh asked with a frown, glancing at Tommy, who'd been listening intently. Josh was a more slick and polished version of his older brother. Natalie had expected him, as a lawyer, to be more formal, but there was no denying he was a Ryan. He had the same dark good looks and the same blue eyes, but Josh's were sharper and a bit more cynical.

"I say we keep digging," Jake said with determination. "These are the first clues we've had in over twenty years. I don't want to stop now." He shrugged. "We know that Rebecca's mom, Margaret Brost, wasn't involved or even in the house when Jesse disappeared. We know she'd been dating a married man named Charlie, whom she was supposed to meet that night. He never showed up, and when she returned to the house, Jesse was gone." Jake frowned, trying to put all the details in order. "We also know that Margaret wrote a ransom note, fearing Charlie was involved in Jesse's disappearance and, because she'd been dating him, she would be, too." Jared blew out a breath, took a sip of coffee. "We also know Margaret was questioned and released simply because there wasn't enough evidence against her. Charlie was waiting for her when she got out, and threatened to harm Rebecca if Margaret ever told the cops anything.

"When Rebecca's story about Jesse's disappearance, and her mother and the mysterious Charlie, hit the papers, we received lots of calls and leads. One was from a woman in Houston, who said her sister used to live in Saddle Falls and might know this Charlie. That's why we headed to Texas in the first place. The woman thought her sister might have dated a prominent married man name Charlie, and it might or might not be the same man."

Jared paused, looked at Rebecca, his eyes filled with love, then glanced around the table. "And the rest you know. It's something, but not nearly enough for us to find Jesse yet. So what do we do? Do we keep digging, knowing this could be just another wild-goose chase, a blind alley that leads nowhere, like all the others in the past? Or do we stop?'' He glanced at his grandfather. "Tommy, it's your call."

Tommy gazed around the table at his grandsons, his heart overflowing with love. At Jake, the eldest and the daredevil, the one he'd worried the most about, married now, with a family on the way.

Then there was Jared, who'd always hid his emotions beneath a quiet, calm facade. Totally responsible and reliable from the time he was a lad, Jared valued the land and family in the same way Tommy himself did. It pleased him to no end, but still brought on worry.

Tommy's gaze shifted to Natalie, who was balancing a stack of plates on her way to the kitchen, and his gaze softened. She'd brought love and laughter to this house again, which had been far too long without it. Hopefully, Jared would recognize the need he had for her, and the love, too. And hopefully Jared would have a wife of his own again—soon. Nothing could please Tommy more.

His gaze shifted to Josh and he grinned. Josh had always been a cool, calm businessman, the one most like Tommy himself. The one who loved the art of the deal, could out-think and outmaneuver anyone around a business table. It was Josh who would handle the reins of Ryan Enterprises after he passed away. The lad was still alone, though, Tommy thought with a frown, simply because Josh didn't trust outsiders enough to let his emotions go. Since Jesse disappeared, Josh had simply stopped showing any emotion. It was as if he buried it, filling his heart with the competition of business. 'Twasn't good, but Tommy couldn't complain, since Josh had handled all of the Ryan businesses with a ruthlessness that doubled their net worth. But Josh was still a worry, for Tommy feared he would never trust a woman enough to let his heart go. Maybe one day when Josh met the right woman, Tommy thought with a sigh, ever hopeful.

His gaze shifted to the end of the table, where Jesse should have sat, and the empty hole in his heart began to ache as it always did when he thought of his youngest grandson.

He'd never stopped worrying, or wondering what had happened to him. Never would.

And he needed to know before he left to meet his maker. He knew he'd never find peace if he didn't.

"We continue," Tommy said firmly, his glance encompassing the entire group. "Jesse is kin, and we need to know what happened to him. We need to bring him home once and for all." The old man's glance was fierce with pride as he looked at his grandsons. "Are we agreed?"

Jake, Jared and Josh glanced at each other, then Jake spoke for all of them. "Yep. We're agreed, Tommy." He smiled at Rebecca, giving her hand a squeeze under the table. "I thought that's what you'd say, so Rebecca and I have booked a flight back to Houston early tomorrow morning. We've got another lead and I'd like to move while the trail's still warm."

"Good. Good." Tommy held up his coffee cup for Natalie to refill it. Her hands were trembling, he noted, glancing up at her with some concern. She'd been bustling in and out of the kitchen, clearing the table, keeping herself busy.

"So, if you don't mind, since we're leaving so early, we're going to stay at the hotel in town. It's closer to the airport." Jake glanced at Josh. "Can we hitch a ride back to town with you?"

Josh flashed a cocky grin. "Yeah, but it'll cost you." He winked at Rebecca. "I get to sit next to your beautiful wife. You can have the back seat."

"Fine, but touch my wife and you're mincemeat, bro," Jake said with a laugh. "Your reputation with women is known far and wide, and I'm not taking any chances. Get your own woman."

"Would anyone like more coffee?" Natalie asked, holding up a fresh pot she'd retrieved from the kitchen. "Or more dessert?"

Jared groaned, then rubbed his stomach. "If I eat another bite I'll explode." He grinned up at her, sliding his arm around her and pulling her close. "That was a fabulous meal, Nat." The low timbre of his voice caused Jake and Josh to exchange curious glances that said more than words.

Natalie flushed, wiggling out of Jared's embrace. She felt so uncomfortable, so nervous, that she couldn't wait for dinner to be over so she could talk to Jared alone.

"Well, boys," Tommy said, getting up from the table. "It's time for the Ryan family tradition." He grinned at Rebecca, then Natalie. "Every holiday, the men of the clan meet in my study to share a brandy and a cigar, but I'm a modern man, and you're welcome to join us if you've a mind."

Rebecca shook her head, then stood up. "Thanks, Tommy, but the mere thought of being around all that cigar smoke is enough to give me morning sickness—again," she added with a groan, laying a hand on her still-flat tummy. She was almost four months pregnant, and the morning sickness that had been plaguing her hadn't stopped. In fact, it had recently spread to both mornings and afternoons.

Jake was on his feet in an instant. "Becca, are you all right?" His worried gaze searched her face and he took her arm, holding it as if she were as fragile as an egg. "Do you need to lie down? Put your feet up?"

Rebecca laughed, laying a hand to his cheek. "I'm pregnant, sweetheart, not handicapped.'' She laughed again. He'd been impossible since he learned she was expecting. ''But I think I would like to lie down for a while.'' She glanced at Tommy. ''If you don't mind?''

''Course not, lass.''

''Then I think I'll just go on back to our house. I haven't even been inside since we got home this morning.'' She and Jake lived in a small coach house behind the main ranch house. It was the house she had lived in when her mother had been the Ryan boys' nanny.

''I'll take you,'' Jake said.

''Jake.'' She sighed. ''I'm perfectly capable of walking a few hundred feet by myself.''

''Tough. I'm going with you—just to be sure.'' He took her arm. ''I'll be back in a few minutes, Tommy.''

''Fine. Fine.'' Tommy beamed at them. ''We'll be in my study.''

Jared stood, too. ''Natalie, would you like some help in the kitchen? I don't need a cigar.''

She shook her head, shooing him toward the doorway. ''No, I'll do better by myself.'' She forced a smile. ''You go enjoy spending time with your brothers.'' She wanted— needed—some time to herself. She hadn't been alone for one moment, not since Raymond's call this morning, and she had to figure out what she was going to say to Jared. She couldn't do that with all these people around.

''Let me just take the last of the dessert plates in at least.'' Jared scooped them up with his large hands even as she began protesting. With a weary sigh, she followed him into the kitchen.

''Jared?''

The tone of her voice had him turning to her. ''What, Nat?'' He looked at her carefully. ''Is something wrong?''

"I...I need to talk to you." She couldn't bear to look into those beautiful eyes. "Privately."

Concerned, he laid a hand to her cheek. "Sure, Nat, sure." His gaze grew worried. "Does this have something to do with what we talked about last night?"

*Last night?* She looked at him blankly for a moment, then remembered that last night he had told her he wanted her to think about making their arrangement more personal.

Was it just last night? It seemed like an eternity ago. Now the only thing on her mind was Raymond's phone call and protecting the boys.

"In a way," she hedged, knowing she couldn't tell him that the possibility of them having any kind of personal relationship was nonexistent now. "I...I just need to talk to you." Her voice wavered, and he stepped closer, resting a hand on her shoulder as he saw the worry in her eyes.

"All right, Nat. Jake and Josh will be leaving soon. Once you put the boys to bed, we'll talk—is that all right?"

Her throat burned with unshed tears, and she nodded, glancing at the clock over the sink. Time seemed to be standing still today. "That's fine."

"Nat?" He lifted her chin so she was forced to look at him. It nearly broke her heart.

"Y-yes?"

"Whatever it is, don't worry, I'm sure we can handle it." He smiled, then bent and brushed his lips against hers, making her heart ache. "Together." He kissed her again, and it took supreme control not to throw her arms around him and hold on, to let it all come pouring out of her. But she couldn't—not now. Not yet.

Natalie glanced at the clock again, vividly aware of every ticking second, knowing that she'd run out of time. No matter what the consequences of her deception, no matter the cost to herself, she had to protect the boys, and Jared was the only one who could help her do that.

# Chapter Eight

Nerves strung as tight as a bowstring, Natalie paced the length of the living room, ignoring the sparks and flames of the fire burning brightly in the hearth. Josh had driven Jake and Rebecca back to the hotel in town, Tommy had gone off to visit friends and Jared was tucking the boys in.

She was absolutely certain it was going to take all night, she decided, casting a quick glance toward the darkened doorway. The boys had been particularly wound up tonight. With the excitement of the holiday, the parade and their uncles' visit, it was to be expected. She just wished her own patience wasn't at an end.

Natalie pressed a hand to her forehead, where a throbbing had started this morning when she'd answered the phone and heard Raymond's voice. The pain had continued all through the day, getting worse and worse by the minute.

"Nat?"

She jumped, whirling to face Jared, who stood in the doorway looking rumpled, tired and more handsome than she'd ever seen him.

"Jared, please, I really need to talk to you. Now." She glanced at him and something in her voice, her eyes, set his nerves on edge. "It's important."

"All right," he said hesitantly, moving forward to take her hand. "Come sit down with me."

She drew her hand away, longing for his touch but knowing she didn't deserve it, couldn't have it—not ever. "No, I can't." She shook her head. She'd held herself together all day, but right now she knew she was on the edge of falling apart, and she couldn't touch him, not until this was over. "I'd rather stand, Jared."

"Fine." Taking a seat in the soft leather chair that had sat in the corner opposite the fireplace for as long as he could remember, Jared simply watched her. "Obviously this must be important."

He had a feeling he knew what this was about—his asking her to think about making their arrangement more personal. He feared he'd spooked her. Judging from the way she'd been acting all day, he was pretty sure of it. He wished he could regret asking her, but he couldn't—didn't. But he wasn't certain he was ready to hear her rejection, either.

"Go ahead, Nat, I'm all ears," he said quietly.

She paced for a moment, twisting her hands together, searching for the right words, the right phrase, trying not to let tears start. They clogged her throat as she finally turned to face him.

"Jared, I don't know how else to say this, but…" She hesitated, swallowed hard, then blinked away the tears she knew she couldn't shed. Not yet. "Jared, I'm afraid that, because of me, the boys are in danger. Serious danger."

His natural protective instincts immediately on alert, Jared leaned forward, fists clenched, fear slowly pouring through his veins like molten lava. He narrowed his gaze on her. "What the hell are you talking about, Natalie?"

"It's a long story."

"Make it short," he ordered, causing her to sigh. She should have expected this.

"Jared, do you remember when you told me you and Kathryn adopted the twins?" Taking a deep breath, Natalie continued pacing, trying to remember that her feelings didn't matter, all that mattered was keeping the boys safe.

"Yeah," he said slowly, trying to figure out what she was getting at. "What about it?"

"Remember you told me the boys' mother had died and their father couldn't take care of them, so he put them up for adoption?"

Impatient, he curled his fingers, then uncurled them. "I remember all of this, but what does it have to do with the boys being in—"

She turned to face him, knowing she couldn't do it any other way. He deserved that much. "Jared, the boys' mother didn't die. She's not dead."

Totally confused, Jared shook his head. "What the hell are you talking about?"

"*I'm* Timmy and Terry's mother." She forced herself to stop and just stand there. "Their natural mother."

Staggered, Jared merely stared at her, totally speechless. He blinked, shifted his gaze, not seeing anything, only hearing her words echoing over and over in his mind.

*Natalie was the boys' natural mother.*

Something akin to rage leaped into his eyes, but he was a man of discipline and banked it down—barely. "I don't believe you." The words were strained with an effort at control.

"Why on earth would I lie about something like this?" Her eyes flashed and she recited information that had been committed to memory. "I gave birth to twin boys five years ago, at Loyola University Medical Center in Maywood, Illinois. Timmy was born first and he weighed four pounds seven ounces. He had an umbilical hernia when he was born that was surgically corrected when he was six weeks old. If you look very closely, you can see the tiny scar." She took a breath, plunged on, ignoring the dangerous light flickering in the depths of Jared's eyes. "Terry was born next and weighed in at four pound, three ounces. He has a birthmark on the top of his skull—you can't see it now because of his hair, but it's in the shape of a crescent moon and cherry-red. The boys stayed in the hospital's neonatal intensive care unit for almost two weeks because they were born almost a month premature. Terry also has a scar on the bottom of his left foot, right near his heel. It's about half an inch long and looks like a squiggly worm. He stepped on a piece of glass right after his second birthday and it required five stitches. All of their medical records, and their hand-and footprints, are on record at the hospital if you want to verify what I'm telling you."

Jared merely stared at her, trying to take it all in.

*Natalie was the twins' mother.*

*Their real mother.*

The implications simply wouldn't sink in. If she was the boys' mother, where had she been all of these years? And what was she doing here now? Why hadn't she told him the truth? Why had she hid it? Lied to him? Deceived him?

Cold fear slid over Jared, settling like a low, aching ball in his gut, causing his skin to chill as his temper flared.

*Natalie had deliberately lied to him and deceived him. Why?*

That was all he kept asking himself. The question echoed over and over in his mind as he looked at her, wondering how this could be the same woman he'd fallen in love with.

*Why would she lie to him?*

He shook his head, trying to concentrate on what she'd told him. Terry's scar. She'd said something about Terry's scar. And Timmy's birthmark. Jared frowned, struggling to put his thoughts in order. During the summer months, he always had the boys' hair cut short because of the heat. But Natalie had arrived in September. The boys' hair had grown out by then, so how could she have known about the scar on the top of Timmy's head?

And Jared had always wondered about the scar on the bottom of Terry's foot. When he'd adopted the boys, Terry already had the scar. Jared had noticed it the first night, when he'd brought the boys home, because like all new fathers, he'd inspected his kids from head to toe.

Realization hit him like a demolition ball, spreading fear, anger and panic through him. His fists clenched and he surged to his feet, not certain what to believe, only knowing his heart had begun to ache in a way he no longer thought possible.

"Natalie," he roared, eyes flashing dangerously, his heart aching with betrayal. "I don't know what the hell kind of a con you think you're pulling—"

"Jared!" Nearly frantic, Natalie grabbed his arm, then shook it, tears swimming in her eyes. "Listen to me!" She tightened her hand on his arm until he looked at her. His gaze was so cold, so angry that she almost recoiled. "Jared, please?" Her voice broke, but he appeared unmoved, and it only hurt more. "This isn't a game or a con, honest. I wouldn't lie to you about something like this." Tears slipped down her cheeks.

"Why not?" he snapped, shaking free of her, trying desperately to ignore the pain slicing through him, ripping him in two. She'd lied to him. Deceived him. Deliberately. Knowingly. Willingly. He'd trusted her, thought he could trust her. Now he knew differently. And dammit, it hurt. "Apparently you've lied to me about everything else. Why wouldn't you lie to me about this?"

The venom in his voice cut her to the quick. Her heart ached so much she pressed her fist to her chest, trying to ease the pain. With a shudder, she took a deep breath.

"Yes, Jared, I have lied to you—"

Bitter bile rose in his throat and he swallowed hard, praying the pain inside would simply go away. He knew better. He'd been down this road before with another woman who'd deliberately lied to him and betrayed him, been down this road and sworn he'd never do it again.

He'd been wrong.

So wrong.

About her.

She was no different than Kathryn. She was worse, in fact, because her actions had been deliberately deceitful.

What a fool he must seem to her, he thought, letting his rage and shame take hold. How the hell had he let another woman make a fool of him? Another woman whom he trusted?

"You've been lying to me since the first day you came to this house, haven't you?"

"Yes," she whispered, trying unsuccessfully to hold back the tears. Taking a deep breath, Natalie tried to remember her feelings didn't matter, all that mattered was keeping the boys safe. "I had no choice."

"Please, spare me," he snapped, venom dripping from his voice. "You deliberately deceived me, the boys and even Tommy, didn't you?" The statement was filled with disgust, but underneath it was a deep layer of pain. She could hear it and was staggered by the depth of hurt she knew she'd inflicted on him.

"Yes," she whispered.

"Why?" he demanded, needing to know why she'd deliberately hurt them. He was an adult; he would be able to lick his wounds and get over his broken heart—eventually, he hoped. But the boys were innocent victims and would be unbearably hurt when they learned the truth of her deception. That angered Jared even further, until the anger was like a white-hot rage boiling inside him. "Why did you deliberately deceive us, Natalie. Why?" His gaze bored into hers, and she knew she couldn't hold back the tears much longer.

She'd hurt him. Had known she would, but hadn't quite been prepared for this, for seeing the light go out of his eyes and pain settle in like it belonged there. Once, he'd looked at her with desire and trust in those beautiful eyes now he looked at her with venom and suspicion, and she wasn't certain she could handle it. Lifting a hand, she swiped at her tears.

"I couldn't tell you the truth, Jared," she whispered, unable to look at him simply because it hurt too much. "I just couldn't." She took a long, shuddering breath, prepared to tell him everything. "About three and a half years ago, my husband—*ex*-husband," she correctly quickly, aware that Jared's body had tensed, his gaze had cooled, his face had hardened. "My ex-husband was discovered embezzling over two million dollars from my father's firm." She stared at the floor, concentrating on what she was saying. "I didn't know it, of course. Raymond had me fooled as well as everyone else, including my father. When my dad learned about the missing funds, he gave Raymond a chance to repay it without pressing charges. Raymond refused, and basically just laughed in my father's face, taunting him, saying my dad would never put his grandchildren's father in jail." Natalie took a deep breath, then continued, glancing briefly at Jared.

"Raymond may have worked for my father for years, but obviously he didn't know my dad very well." Pausing to take a breath, she slipped her trembling hands in her jeans pockets so she wouldn't reach for Jared. She wanted him to hold her right now, hold her and tell her everything was all right. Looking at him, she knew nothing would ever be all right again.

"My father pressed charges against Raymond. He didn't have a choice." She managed a watery smile. "If you knew my father, you'd understand." She shrugged. "He'd worked a lifetime building a successful contracting business and reputation. He subsequently learned that Raymond had been taking kickbacks—bribes—in order to award business to vendors. It was a nightmare, Jared, just a nightmare," she said with a sad shake of her head.

"My father was both humiliated and ashamed, and I felt guilty. Guilty because it was my husband, after all, who'd done these horrible things to my father." Lifting a hand, she brushed away tears, wishing she could brush away the shame. "When my father finally realized the extent of Raymond's business dealings, well, that's when he pressed charges, and my ex-husband was arrested."

Taking a slow, deep breath, and then forcing it out of her aching lungs, Natalie pushed her hair off her face, then continued. "Raymond wanted me to bail him out, but I refused. The twins had just turned two and I'd realized long before that that our marriage was over. I realized I'd never really known Raymond. He conned me just like he had my father. But then again, he'd had years of experience. He kept calling me, asking me—begging me—to bail him out. I kept refusing. He went from begging to threatening." She ran her hands up and down her suddenly chilled arms. "I guess a friend bailed him out because one day I came home from the grocery store and he was sitting in the kitchen.

He asked me—begged me—to go to my father and ask him to drop the charges.'' The memories were so painful, she had to stop for a moment, pressing a hand to her forehead, then forced herself to continue in spite of the nausea that was threatening. "I absolutely refused. I was ashamed of what he'd done, ashamed that he was my husband, and more than anything else, ashamed that he was the twins' father. I'd made a very bad mistake in judgment and because of it…'' Her voice hitched, and she pressed a hand to her mouth to stop the sobs, struggling for control. She took another deep breath. "Because I'd made a fatal error in judgment, my poor father and my precious sons would suffer.'' Slowly, she lifted her gaze to Jared's. He was watching her intently, quietly, not moving. Just watching. But his eyes were glazed with something she couldn't identify, and his fists were still clenched tightly at his sides.

"Raymond never had much interest in the twins. They were merely an inconvenience to him, but he knew they were my life.'' Her throat clogged again, but she forced herself to continue. "Raymond told me if I didn't ask my father to drop the charges—if I didn't *make* him do so— I'd live to regret it.'' Natalie shut her eyes, which were swimming with tears she could no longer hold back. She shook her head, desperately trying to hang on. "I didn't take him seriously,'' she whispered, her voice strained. Still in denial, she shook her head. "It was another fatal error in judgment on my part.'' Her voice had dropped to barely a whisper.

"Two days later Raymond stole the twins from their play group and disappeared.'' The tears came flooding now, coursing down her cheeks. Natalie didn't bother to wipe them away. "That was the last time I saw my boys.'' She sniffled, pressing a hand to her heart again because it ached so. "I was frantic—terrified. Raymond was obviously desperate. I had no idea what he might do to the boys. I thought—I actually thought I might lose my mind from grief, from fear, from loss.'' Now her own fists clench and she began to pace again, unable to stand still. ''I swore I'd find my children, swore that I wouldn't let Raymond get away with this. My babies were innocent, and he'd used them as pawns in a vicious game of revenge and intimidation.'' Natalie paused in front of the fire, blindly watching it, lost in her own thoughts.

Jared stared at her, stunned, his emotions torn, his heart aching for her. Part of him wanted to go to her, to take her in his arms and hold her, to protect her from the pain that was so visible it was like a living thing crawling over her, touching every inch of her.

He couldn't bear to see the fear in her eyes, hear it in her voice, couldn't bear the thought that someone had violated her in such a way, bullied her, threatened her with something that was almost unspeakable.

The white-hot rage that had coursed through him, hazing his vision and tightening his fists, shifted to her ex-husband, to the man who had stolen her children and put her through hell. The urge to put his fist through the nearest wall was strong, but Jared resisted it. He'd learned long ago that neither anger nor violence solved anything. But he wasn't so controlled that the temptation wasn't there.

What kind of man stole his own children for revenge? he wondered.

What kind of man had so little regard for two innocent lives that he could rip toddlers from their mother and then put them up for adoption? To a man to whom family meant everything, such actions were incomprehensible.

But he was also wary because Natalie had deliberately lied to him from the very first day, and he still didn't know why.

The unanswered question was like a dagger pointed at his heart, stopping him from taking any action.

"My father died of a heart attack less than a year later," she said softly, turning from the fire to face Jared, her eyes glazed with tears. "He blamed himself for the boys' abduction. I told him repeatedly it wasn't his fault, that he had no control over Raymond's actions. No one did. No one knew how dangerous or delusional Raymond had become. No one could have predicted that he'd use the boys as pawns to get back at me—at us." She shook her head. "My father couldn't take the guilt or the stress. When Raymond abducted the boys everything came out. His embezzlement became public knowledge. Dad's customers apparently lost confidence in him and took their business elsewhere. He had to file for bankruptcy." Sniffling, Natalie began pacing again. "I think that was the last straw for my father. The stress of the situation caused him to have a massive heart attack." She lifted her gaze to Jared's, her eyes stricken, her heart in tatters. "He died instantly," she said, her voice a whisper of agony.

Jared's arms ached and his fists clenched. He wanted to go to her, to hold her, to comfort her, but he couldn't. His own heart was aching over her betrayal and he simply couldn't seem to get past it.

He watched as Natalie took a moment to compose herself, rubbing her chilled arms again, pacing the length of the living room as if needing to move, to do something so she wouldn't simply collapse in a heap.

"After all Dad's expenses, there wasn't much left, but I used every last penny I had to search for the boys. I hired a private investigator and I've spent the last three years of my life trying to find them."

"And you did." His voice sounded so strained, he almost didn't recognize it. Emotions churned through him, tearing him in two. He couldn't ever remember being so conflicted before. Couldn't remember ever feeling so torn up inside.

"Yes." Natalie forced herself to hold his gaze. "I found my sons."

Stunned, staggered, Jared merely stared at her, wondering how she'd survived.

Losing her children... Jared dragged a hand through his hair, glanced at her, saw that her face had drained of all color. He wanted to go to her, yet his heart simply wouldn't allow it

She'd lost her children! It was difficult to comprehend. The mere thought was utterly incomprehensible. He knew how he felt about the boys, knew how he'd feel if they suddenly disappeared from his life.

He'd go mad, because the boys *were* his life.

There was no end to the depth of his love for the twins. None. Losing them was so incomprehensible he couldn't even begin to fathom how Natalie had coped.

But he didn't trust what he was feeling right now. Not for her.

She'd deliberately tricked him.

Broken his heart by betraying it.

"Why didn't you just tell me the truth?" he asked quietly, so quietly she wanted to put her head in her hands and weep.

"I couldn't, Jared. I simply couldn't." Her breathing felt labored and her chest actually hurt from tension. "Only hours after the boys disappeared Raymond called. He wanted to gloat, but he also warned me that he'd be watching me, and that if I ever tried to find him or the boys, he'd make them pay." Reluctantly, she looked up at Jared. "I couldn't take the chance, not after he'd abducted them. I simply couldn't risk telling you the truth. I couldn't tell anyone the truth—that I'd finally found my children. I simply wouldn't risk it.'' She wouldn't apologize for trying to protect her children, not after her failure to do so had caused them all such life-altering grief. She looked at Jared, wondering if he would ever understand, if he'd even try.

She knew she'd hurt him, knew that her deliberate lies had shaken his faith, his trust in her. But he had to see she had her reasons—good reasons. She never would have betrayed him otherwise. Never. She loved him, deeply, desperately. He was, she knew, the finest man she'd ever met.

And she had to do something to try to make this right between them before she told him the rest.

She took a step closer, wanting to bridge the distance between them, then froze when he stepped back, making it clear that lines had been drawn.

She sighed, feeling the ache that coursed through her, knowing she deserved this, but still wanting him, loving him, all the same.

Jared's mind raced with questions that had no answers. ''Natalie, didn't the authorities try to find Raymond? I mean, kidnapping your own children is a crime.'' He was trying to make sense of everything she'd told him, trying to understand, but it was difficult to cut through the pain and anger to think clearly.

''Of course. I contacted the authorities the moment I realized he'd abducted the boys. In addition to the embezzlement charges, they added numerous other charges against him, including kidnapping, extortion, fleeing in order to avoid prosecution.'' She shrugged, her gaze sad. ''But it's been three years, Jared. Raymond's trail had grown cold and there are other cases, other missing children. The authorities simply stopped making Raymond a priority. But I never did. I couldn't.''

''Didn't you try to find him?''

Understanding his questions, she tried to be patient, when all she wanted to do was plead with him to protect the boys. He was her only hope to keep them safe, to keep them here. "Jared, like I said, I didn't have much money left, and my focus was on finding the boys. I used every last penny I had to pay the private investigator to do that. I simply didn't have any more funds to look for Raymond as well."

The picture was now becoming much clearer. "So that's how you knew I'd adopted the boys. A private investigator?"

"Yes." She wrapped her arms around herself, suddenly chilled. "He worked diligently for the past three years, but found mostly false leads and dead ends until the beginning of September." She glanced up at Jared. "He saw the article in the *Saddle Falls News* that Rebecca wrote. There was a picture of the twins in it."

Jared nodded. He remembered when the photo had been taken. He hadn't been happy about it, but since the story was about the entire history of the Ryan family, and it was something Tommy felt strongly about and actually endorsed, Jared hadn't had the heart to say no.

Now he sorely regretted his actions.

"Once Harry saw the picture, he felt certain it was the boys, but he wanted to be sure, so he flew here to Nevada and checked the school records." She shrugged. "You needed the boys' birth certificates to register them for school."

Jared frowned. "We were given new birth certificates when the adoption was finalized."

"I know." Natalie took a deep breath. "But the new birth certificates still had their fingerprints on them. Harry had a copy of the boys' fingerprints from the hospital where they were born. When the fingerprints matched, we knew for sure it was Timmy and Terry.''

"You started this conversation by saying the boys were in danger." His voice was viciously cold, detached. "Why did you say that?"

A shiver raced over her and she began to tremble in earnest. "Jared, I don't know how…I don't know…" She dragged a hand through her hair, wishing she could change what she had to tell him. "This morning when I was getting the boys ready for the parade, Raymond called me."

The tension that had been clawing at his insides felt like razor blades, sharp and deadly. Jared's gaze narrowed and the white-hot rage flared up again, out of control, nearly consuming him. He took a step closer to her, causing Natalie to take a step back. "He called here? At my home?"

Miserable, Natalie could only nod. "Jared, he's found us." A sob broke loose. "He knows I've found the boys, and I'm afraid he's going to do something to harm them." She took a step closer now, no longer caring about her own pain or pride, caring only that the boys would be protected, safe. "Jared, please, no matter how you feel about me, or what I've done, you *have* to protect the boys." She reached for him, catching the front of his shirt with her hands and holding on even when he made a move to step back. "Please, Jared. You have no idea what he's capable of. No idea how insane he really is." She glanced up at him, her face stricken, her heart broken, nerves tattered. "Jared, you're my only hope this time. My only hope to protect the boys."

He glanced down at her, feeling as if someone had ripped out his heart. "How can you even ask such a thing of me?" He grabbed her hands, shook her. "After all this time, don't you know me at all?" His voice shuddered with pain and disgust that she didn't know him enough to know he'd die before he'd let anyone hurt his children. "Do you think I'd let *anyone* hurt or threaten my children?"

"They're *my* children, Jared," she said softly, but she wasn't certain her words even penetrated his flash flood of anger.

"This is my home, Natalie." His voice was husky with the force of his emotions. "And those are my children. They're Ryans through and through, and no one—I repeat, no one—will ever hurt, harm or threaten a Ryan child again." Glaring down at her he stepped closer until his toes bumped her, glaring down at her.

In spite of how he felt about her right now, it didn't alter the fact that he needed her help, needed to find out what Raymond had said, in the hopes of figuring out what the man had planned. And like it or not, Natalie was the only one who could help him do that.

"Now, I want you to tell me exactly what Raymond said this morning." Jared paused, his lips pursed tightly. "Every single thing, even if you don't think it's important. Do you understand?"

The intensity in his voice, in his body, was almost frightening, but she'd forgotten how fiercely protective and prideful the Ryans were.

"Y-yes." Natalie shivered.

"Come and sit down." His voice was still cold, but had gentled a bit. Taking her hand, he ignored the spark he always felt whenever he touched her, ignored it knowing he could never again trust her, or what he felt for her. Not after she'd deceived him. His heart ached with love for her, but he knew he couldn't trust what he was feeling now, any more than he could trust her.

He led her to the leather chair, then walked to the sideboard to pour her a brandy. "Drink this," he ordered, handing her the glass. "It will calm you down."

She sipped the potent liquor, making a face as it burned a path down her throat. She set the glass on the table next to her.

"Feel better?" He wanted to lay a hand on her cheek and tell her not to worry, that he wasn't going to let anything happen to her or the boys. But he couldn't, not now.

"Y-yes." She nodded, sliding back in the leather chair and tucking her legs under her. "I was just getting ready to leave for the parade this morning when—"

"What time was it exactly? Do you remember?" Jared stood in front of her, alert and on edge.

Her brows drew together. "About ten I think. I had just put the turkey in the oven."

Jared nodded in acknowledgment. "What did Raymond say exactly?"

Natalie's eyes closed and she recounted the conversation for him, as exact as she could remember it.

"He actually said he'd be seeing you and the boys?" Jared deliberately tried to cool the rage stalking him. He knew he had to think clearly and carefully, and he couldn't do that if his mind was clouded with emotion. Deliberately, he erased everything from his brain, ignored the deep ache in his heart and concentrated only on her words and what she was relating.

"Yes," she whispered, taking the glass again when he held it toward her. She wrapped her hands around it as if only to stop their trembling.

Jared's mind skipped to several possibilities. "Natalie, who knows you're here?"

She thought for a moment, then shook her head. "No one. Absolutely no one. I couldn't risk having anyone know." She paused. "Except for Harry Powers, the private investigator who found the boys." She caught the look on Jared's face. "Oh no, Jared." Frightened at what he was thinking, she slid forward in the chair. "He would never have told Raymond. He's a good, honest man who's worked the past year without getting a penny in fees." She shook her head. "No, Jared, he would never have told Raymond." She would never believe that Harry could betray her, not after he'd known the heartache and hardship she'd gone through trying to find her boys. "Harry was head of security for my father's company for many, many years. He considered my dad a friend. I won't believe he'd betray me." So many people had, she couldn't believe it of Harry, too.

Jared dragged a hand through his hair, pacing the length of the room, his mind whirling. "Okay, is there anyone else, Nat, anyone else who knows you're here, or that you found the boys?"

"No. There's no one."

"Raymond had to find out where they were, where you were somehow."

"Jared, I don't have a clue. Honestly. I don't. I never would have done anything that would give me or the boys away." Her fingers tightened on the brandy snifter. "I've lived in fear that Raymond would discover I'd found the boys. That's why I deceived you, Jared. That's why I lied to you. That's the only reason. To protect the boys."

His heart desperately wanted to believe her, but his mind simply couldn't get past the knowledge that she'd deliberately deceived him. He couldn't sort it out now. At the moment, he had to do whatever was necessary to protect his children.

He turned to her, meeting her gaze and holding it. "Are you lying to me now, Natalie?" he asked slowly. For a moment, she drew back as if he'd slapped her, then her face crumpled and she broke down in tears. Jared ached to hold her, knowing she was frightened, knowing she was alone, so alone. Knowing she was desperately hurt. But he couldn't do it. Couldn't make himself take that step, not after what she'd done. He couldn't trust her. And he couldn't trust his feelings. So he'd simply go on his instincts and the facts, in the same way he'd been doing for the past three years.

"No, Jared," she finally managed to whisper, wiping her eyes with her hand. "I'm not."

Jared continued to stare at her for a long, silent moment. She stared back, trying to read his thoughts. But it was as if an invisible shutter had dropped down, cutting her off.

Banishing her from his heart.

She wasn't certain she could feel anything any more, but the ache in her heart was real. Desperate, she set the glass down and stood up, fearing her legs wouldn't hold her. She was physically and emotionally drained.

"Jared, what are you going to do?"

"What I've always done," he said firmly, striding toward the doorway. "Protect my children."

"Jared." Her voice stopped him and he turned to her.

"What?"

"W-what do you want me to do?"

"I think, Natalie," he said slowly, letting his gaze meet hers until she shivered again, "that you've done more than enough."

With that, Jared strode out of the living room, leaving her standing there, miserable, heartsick, staring after him.

# Chapter Nine

Weary with fatigue, not knowing what else to do with herself, Natalie crept into the boys' room. They were sound asleep. Terry had his fists jammed under his pillow, his legs tangled in the sheets. Timmy was on his back, a pillow half over his face, one leg over the covers, one leg under.

Looking at them, Natalie felt her heart ache. She loved them so. But so did Jared, she thought sadly. She'd never once doubted that.

They both loved the boys.

And she'd thought they might have a chance at loving each other.

Now she knew her actions had killed any love or affection Jared had ever felt for her. She'd read it in his face, his eyes, in the coldness that radiated off of him in waves.

And she wasn't certain he'd ever be able to forgive her. Nor was she certain she could ever forgive herself.

Holding back a sob, Natalie kissed her sons' foreheads, then spent a moment stroking their silky hair. It had been so long since she'd felt free—free from stress, from pain, rom fear. All she wanted, all she'd ever wanted, was to aise her boys in peace and safety. To love and mother hem. To give them all the stability and security she'd had growing up.

But that simple option in life had been taken away from her because she'd made an error in judgment and married a man who'd fooled her.

She'd been so young, so gullible, she acknowledged with a sigh, and unfortunately, she'd thought she'd loved Raymond.

Now, compared to the depth of feeling she felt for Jared—for the unmitigated joy she felt every time he was in the room, every time he was near, or touched her, or kissed her—she finally knew what true love was.

She'd been one of the lucky ones to find it.

But she'd lost it.

Because once again she'd made an error in judgment.

Heartsick, Natalie stood in the darkened bedroom, watching her beautiful sons. All she'd ever wanted was for them to be safe and happy.

Maybe now they would be.

But she had no idea how she and Jared would finally settle this issue.

She loved the boys totally, completely, unconditionally.

She was their mother by birth and by blood.

But Jared also loved them totally, completely and unconditionally.

He was their father, maybe not by birth or blood, but in all the ways that truly mattered.

Any man could father a child, but it took a very special man to be a great daddy. Jared was one of those rare men.

And she loved him so.

And she'd lost him.

Natalie knew he'd probably never forgive her for deceiving him, never forgive her for lying.

She was going to lose him—lose him before she ever really had him.

And it hurt so much, she didn't know how to stop the pain.

Totally exhausted, she grabbed the small afghan at the bottom of Terry's bed, wrapped it around herself, then lay down on the floor between the boys' beds, wanting only to be near them. She needed to be close to them in order to be absolutely certain they were safe.

Natalie let out a long, slow breath, then closed her eyes, praying that when she woke up, this horribly long nightmare would finally be over.

It took Jared less than two hours to round up Josh, Jake and Tommy and brief them on the situation. Their reaction, as Jared had expected, was just about the same as his.

"No one threatens the Ryans," Josh said, pacing the length of the kitchen, his fists clenched, ready for a fight. The cool, calm lawyer was gone, replaced by a man of fierce pride and familial loyalty. He'd stripped off his suit jacket and rolled up the sleeves of his dress shirt, more than ready to take on the world to protect his own.

"You got that right," Jake concurred, doing a little pacing of his own, his jaw clenched, his fists flexing.

"Words, lads," Tommy said, putting on a fresh pot of coffee, knowing it was going to be a very long night. "Merely words. They won't help us find this man. We need to have a plan." Tommy pulled out a chair and sat down heavily, leaning his cane against the table. "I've put in a call to some friends of mine, friends who were very useful to me after Jesse disappeared."

"Bodyguards," Jake said with an approving nod, remembering when his grandfather had told him that, right after Jesse disappeared, the men he believed to be new ranch hands had really been bodyguards, hired to protect him and his remaining brothers.

Tommy Ryan would take no chances with his family ever again.

"In a manner of speaking," Tommy said with a smile. "There'll be six men here within the hour to guard the perimeter of the ranch. No one will be able to get onto our land without one of them knowing about it. Two more will be stationed right outside the front door, two more out back. Each is licensed to carry a firearm and will be fully prepared to do whatever is necessary to protect the security of this family." He paused, letting his words sink in before continuing. "Now, as for the little lads. Fortunately, they're out of school for a few days because of the holiday so we don't have to worry about them leaving the ranch. At least not for now. We can protect them best here on our own property." He shrugged. "And if we've not solved this problem by the time the little lads have to return to school, well then, the boys will either have a new friend take them to school, or they'll have a family vacation they didn't plan on." He smiled, confident that, no matter what, he would protect his grandchildren. Never again would someone destroy what was his.

Jared nodded in approval. Nearly desolate over Natalie's deception, he knew he couldn't think about it now. At the moment he had to focus on keeping the boys safe and finding Raymond. But now that he'd had a chance to think about the situation, something was eating at him.

"Tommy, I don't understand how Raymond could have found Natalie. She claims she didn't tell anyone, except the private investigator she'd hired, where she was going. He's the one who found the boys for her, so I don't know that he'd give them up.''

"Do you believe her?" Jake asked quietly.

Jared blew out a breath. "I don't know," he said honestly, looking at his older brother. "I don't know what to believe anymore." Everything he'd believed about Natalie until now had been a lie. All lies. He felt as if he'd been standing on shifting sand until he'd been tossed totally off balance.

"It doesn't make sense," Josh said, filling the coffee mugs and retrieving cream from the refrigerator. "If Natalie knew Raymond was a little nuts, knew that he'd come after the boys if she found them, why on earth would she tell anyone?" He shook his head, then carried the mugs to the table. "Seems to me she'd keep it to herself to protect the boys. I don't believe she'd do anything to hurt her own children."

Jared's head snapped up when Josh said "her own children." Then he realized it was a fact he was going to have to get used to. *The boys were Natalie's.*

His jaw tightened. But they were also his and there was no way in hell he was giving them up—ever—not without one helluva fight. Jared rubbed his hands over his face, his mind a blur. He couldn't think about that.

Maybe once he had the Raymond situation under control, then he'd be able to deal with the situation with Natalie.

"Nay, I don't, either, Son." Tommy glanced at Jared. "It's clear Natalie loves the boys from the bottom of her heart. She lied to protect them, as a mother should," he said with an approving nod.

Stunned, Jared glanced sharply at his grandfather. "Tommy, you certainly can't condone what she did?"

Tommy looked at him with a slight smile. "Condone?" He thought about it for a moment. "That's an odd word,

Son. I don't claim to know Natalie's mind, but I'd say she did what any mother would do to protect her children.'' Cocking his head, he held his grandson's gaze. "Are you telling me you wouldn't lie or do whatever was necessary to protect those precious babes and ensure their safety?"

Tommy's words hit at the heart of him, and Jared felt himself flush, feeling slightly ashamed. "No, Tommy, I'm not telling you that." He blew out a breath, wondering if perhaps he was letting his own bruised ego and aching heart blind him to the circumstances that had caused Natalie to deceive him—circumstances that now, with Tommy's spin on them, seemed almost understandable. Even acceptable. "I'd do anything to protect my sons." It was a fact, and he wasn't going to deny it.

"Aye," Tommy said with a nod. "But don't think family pride, protection, or loyalty is a Ryan exclusive. In my memory, there's nothing more fierce than a mother protecting her young."

"I know, but—"

"Whatever the case," Tommy said, not letting Jared finish, "it's clear she loves the lads more than anything, and I'd not believe she'd harm them at all. Nay, not at all. Not ever." Tommy glanced at Jared, understanding his misery, wanting to ease his burden. "'Twas a brave thing she did, Son," he said softly, tempering his words with a pat on Jared's hand. "Coming here, hiding who she was so she could be near the lads." Tommy nodded knowingly. "A brave thing, indeed. She knew the risks, knew what would happen if Raymond found out. Knew, too, what would happen if you found out, but she took her chances just to claim her boys. In my mind she's a brave, remarkable woman." Tommy paused, then added softly, "Like your mother."

Jared shut his eyes. He didn't want to hear this, didn't want to hear that Natalie had been brave or that she was remarkable. He'd thought those things as well. *Before*. Before he'd learned she'd betrayed him, lied to him.

But was it only to protect the boys? he wondered. And if so, why did it hurt so much?

"Yeah, bro, I don't think she'd tell anyone, either. Why would she want to put the boys at risk?" Jake shook his head. "Raymond may have known all along where the boys were," he said with a frown, trying to put the puzzle pieces together. "He's the one who put them up for adoption, right? He must have known Kathryn's father before that, otherwise I don't think he would have risked doing something that stupid." Jake shrugged, glancing at the stove to see if the coffee was ready. "Raymond probably knew where the boys were all along."

"Yeah, but knowing where the boys were didn't guarantee Raymond would know Natalie would find them or come here," Josh interrupted. "Even if Raymond knew where the boys were, that doesn't explain how he knew Natalie had found them."

Thoughtfully, Tommy sipped his coffee, then slowly set it down, glancing at Jared. "Maybe 'twasn't Natalie who told someone she'd found the boys." His brows rose in question. "Is it possible, lad, that it could have been you?" he asked gently.

All eyes turned to Jared, and he stared at them mutely for a moment.

"Me?" Angered, he felt the word explode from his mouth. "I haven't told anyone Natalie was—oh God." Jared swore softly under his breath, then shook his head with a guttural moan. He scrubbed his hands across his face, cursing himself and his stupidity. "I don't believe it." He blew out a breath, the reality of his actions hitting him like a sledgehammer.

"What? What!" Jake demanded impatiently, stopping his pacing to glare at his brother.

"Kathryn." Jared's gaze shifted to his brothers, then his grandfather, and he groaned again. "You know how Kathryn calls once a year or so to pretend she cares about the boys?"

"Aye, you've told us she's done this in the past, lad," Tommy said with a frown. "Although what her purpose is still eludes me. The lass never had an ounce of caring or loyalty to family or the little lads." He couldn't hide the disapproval in his voice.

"I know, Tommy." Jared knew better than anyone. "Kathryn called me about a month ago, and I had to gloat, to rub it in that we were doing very well without her. That I'd hired a new nanny the boys adored."

"Bingo," Josh said. "This all makes sense. If Raymond knew Kathryn's father, it's a good bet he knew her, too. Maybe she reports to Raymond anything interesting every time she calls to check on the boys. Maybe this time she reported that you had a wonderful new nanny—"

"Named Natalie," Jared interjected miserably. He pushed his hands through his hair, then glanced at his family. "So I blew it. I'm the one who actually tipped Raymond off." Feeling miserable, Jared cursed himself again. "So what do we do now? How do we find Raymond?"

"That's easy." Jake grinned. "Through Kathryn."

"She's not just going to give us the information out of the goodness of her heart," Jared said, not liking the idea of having to deal with his ex-wife again.

"I don't believe she ever had a heart," Josh said, turning a chair around and then sinking down on it and helping himself to a cup of coffee. He poured a second one for Jared and slid it across the table to him.

"Not through her heart," Jake said with a smile. "But

through the pocketbook. The only language that woman has ever understood.''

"I'll deal with Kathryn," Jared said, reaching for his coffee, wanting, needing something to jolt his system. The coffee tasted as bitter as his guilt. Guilt that he'd brought this on and possibly exposed both Natalie and his sons to this lunatic Raymond. "I want to handle this myself," he said firmly, aware that his brothers and grandfather had exchanged worried glances.

"Do you think that's wise, lad?" Tommy asked casually. "Wouldn't it be better if you stayed here with the boys and let your brothers take care of this? They have no history with her, and she has no ax to grind with them."

Jared shook his head, getting to his feet. "No," he said firmly. "This is my problem, my family that's threatened. I'm the one who caused the problem, so I'm the one who needs to fix it."

"Do you know where she is?" Jake asked with a frown.

Jared nodded. "She's been living in Vegas since she left me. She wanted to be close to her father."

"And all the action," Josh added with a knowing look. He'd never liked Kathryn's high-flying lifestyle. Nor Kathryn.

Jared glanced at his brothers, saw the concern on their faces and loved them for it. But he knew that, on this, he wouldn't budge. "I need to do this for myself," he said to Jake and Josh, waiting until they gave reluctant nods of approval.

"We'll stay here with Nat and the boys," Josh said, glancing at Jake again. "Just to be on the safe side."

Jared's glance shifted to Tommy, and a look of understanding passed between them. Only Tommy, who'd gone through the agony of Jesse's disappearance, would know and understand that Jared had to make certain, had to be sure he protected his children.

"I'll be careful," Jared said quietly, patting his grandfather's shoulder. "I promise."

"Aye, that you will, Son. I've not raised a fool. But just remember, the law is there for a reason." Tommy got to his feet, retrieved his cane. "And it won't do the lads any good to have you locked in jail. So mind your step," he said sternly, giving his grandson a firm poke with the tip of his cane. "Mind your step, is all."

"I will, Tommy." Feeling an overwhelming rush of love and loyalty, Jared clamped a hand on his grandfather's shoulder, amazed at how strong, how broad it still was.

"Come on now, lad, I'll walk you out and give you a few pointers."

Jake stepped forward, stuck out his hand. "Call if you need us, bro."

Josh got to his feet, a worried look on his face. "No matter what, you keep in touch."

"I will." Jared hesitated, glanced at his family, feeling a surge of love. This was what families were all about, he thought. Being there to help one another in times of crisis.

Who had helped Natalie? a small voice inside his head whispered. Who had helped her when she was left alone, her children kidnapped, her money gone, with nowhere to turn?

He knew the answer, and he didn't much like it.

No one.

She'd had no family, no one to look out for her or the boys, no one to protect her. The thought caused a hard ball of pain to settle low in his gut.

She'd been alone, victimized and frightened, at the mercy of a madman who couldn't have cared less about her or the boys. Jared's fists clenched impotently and he vowed that no matter what, this night would not end until he was certain, absolutely certain, that neither Natalie nor the boys would ever be victims again.

He shook his brother's hand. "Jake, I know you've got an early morning flight—"

"It's canceled," Jake said firmly. "Family comes first. Rebecca and I aren't going anywhere until this matter is settled."

"Ditto for me, bro," Josh said, picking up his mug and draining it. "I've put the night manager at the hotel on notice that I'm going to be out for the rest of the night, possibly longer." He shrugged, then flashed a wicked, charming grin. "That's why I pay him. To handle things when I'm not there." He clamped a hand on Jared's shoulder. "Go do what you need to do. Jake and I will hold down the fort here." Josh gave his brother's shoulder a squeeze. "No one will get past us, bro. Natalie and the boys will be safe."

Jared managed a smile, knowing his brothers would die before letting any harm come to his family.

*His family.*

He blinked, wondering when he'd started thinking of Natalie as his family.

Right about the time he'd fallen in love with her.

*He loved her.*

*The knowledge that he'd fallen in love with Natalie staggered him and he wondered how he could have been so blind. From the moment he'd laid eyes on her, from the moment she'd stepped into his life—his boys' lives, every moment had been leading to this. He knew it in his heart, but his mind had simply refused to accept or acknowledge it.*

*But now, with his family's welfare at stake, he knew that he couldn't deny his own feelings any longer.*

*Not for Natalie.*

*He loved her.*

*And at the moment, he had no idea what to do about it. But he didn't have to worry about it at the moment. At the moment, all he had to think about was that his brothers would protect his family and keep them safe.*

He smiled at his brothers. "Thanks, guys."

Tommy nudged him along. "Come, lad, I've got a few tips to pass along, as I mentioned." Whistling softly to disguise his worry, the old man ambled down the long marble foyer toward the front door, pausing just as he reached it. "Lad." He turned to Jared, the worry clear in his crystal blue eyes. "I understand your need to do this, but you need to be careful as well."

Jared smiled, his heart filled with overwhelming love for his grandfather. "I already promised I'd be careful."

Tommy leveled him with a gaze. "Sometimes it's difficult to be careful when emotions are in turmoil."

"I'm fine." He hated how cold and clipped his voice sounded, but he didn't think he could talk about Natalie and what had happened yet. He needed to take care of this business, to make sure she and the boys were safe, before he could analyze his own feelings about what had happened, or even attempt to make sense of it.

"You know, Son," Tommy began slowly. "It comes to mind what I would have done had we found Jesse."

Jared frowned, not understanding. "What does finding Jesse have to do with the Natalie?"

"Everything, Son." Tommy grinned. "Simply everything." Cocking his head, the old man held his grandson's gaze. "If we'd have found Jesse, would you have had it that we not claim him, not let him know he was a Ryan? But simply leave him be?"

"Of course not," Jared snapped, not seeing the correlation. "Jesse was—is a Ryan. Always was, always will be. We'd do everything we could to claim him, to let him know who he was." The thought of doing anything else appalled him.

"Aye, of course," Tommy said with a nod. "And so Natalie's boys were always hers. *Her family.* All she had in the world. As we would have claimed Jesse from wherever or whoever had him, Natalie came to claim her family, as well." Tommy shrugged, knowing the lad would need time to digest this. "You can't fault her for that, Son. Not at all."

The thought simmered in Jared's mind, and he realized Tommy had a point. They would no more have walked away from Jesse had they found him then Natalie could have walked away from the boys, pretending she'd never found them.

Such a thing was simply not an option.

"But she deliberately lied to me, deceived me—all of us." Jared shook his head, his emotions torn, his thoughts confused. Had he been too harsh? Had he been too judgmental? He honestly didn't know anymore, not when he put himself in Natalie's place, not even when he realized what he'd do had he found his brother.

"Aye, trust is a fragile thing, Son, as is love. Now family, that's where strength lies." Tommy patted Jared's shoulder. "She was protecting her children, her family, from a madman, in the only way she knew how. I can't fault her for it, for I can't say that I wouldn't have done the same thing had we found Jesse." Tommy waited a beat. "Can you, Son? Can you say you'd do differently, knowing what was at stake?" He held his grandson's gaze for a long, silent moment. "And I'd make no apologies for it, either," Tommy added firmly.

Jared merely stared at his grandfather.

"Okay, Son, off with you now," Tommy said, before Jared could sort through his thoughts enough to offer a response. "Do what you must, knowing your family is here, behind you, always. Remember, it's always wise to use your head instead of your fists." Tommy grinned suddenly. "But know your fists are an option."

Tommy pulled open the front door, pleased to see the two men standing in the shadows. "And mind your step, Son." He clamped a hand on Jared's arm, heavy enough to remind the lad of what he expected. "Mind your step as you go."

With a sigh, Jared rubbed his weary eyes, then glanced in his rearview mirror. It had taken him almost three hours round-trip to drive to Las Vegas and track Kathryn down. It had been a very costly visit, but well worth the ten thousand dollar check he'd left in her hands, he thought grimly, slowly pulling into the long, winding drive that led to the main ranch house.

Stifling a yawn, he parked the car, then stepped out with a frown, wondering why the kitchen light was on. It was almost dawn. His brothers and Tommy should have been asleep long ago, right after he'd called and told them what had happened.

Nerves still thrumming, Jared quietly let himself into the kitchen, grateful that Ditka and Ruth were sleeping outside in their doghouse, or their barking would wake up the whole house.

Weary, he stopped short when he spotted Natalie sitting at the kitchen table, her hands hugging a mug of coffee.

"Nat, what are you doing up?" He shut the door quietly behind him, then took a deep breath before turning to face her. He'd spent most of the three-hour drive thinking about what she'd told him, and what Tommy had said, and now he had a few things to say himself.

But he'd been hoping to have some time to sort through things, to say them in the proper order. He'd never expected her to still be up and awake.

"Waiting for you," she said quietly, letting her gaze feast on him.

"It's late," he said unnecessarily, slipping off his leather jacket and hanging it on a peg by the back door. "You didn't have to wait up."

"Yes," she corrected firmly. "I did." She glanced down at her coffee, then drew the front of her robe tighter. "Your brothers told me where you went." Her worried gaze searched his. Other than looking drawn and tired, he didn't seem any the worse for wear, she thought in relief. She'd feared that if he actually found Raymond, they might come to blows. Not that she didn't think Jared would come out on top, but she wasn't certain of Raymond's mental state, and fighting was always a dicey proposition.

"Got any more of that coffee?" He headed toward the cabinet to get a cup.

"I just made a fresh pot." She waited while he poured himself a cup before speaking again. "Are we going to make small talk or are you going to tell me what happened?" Fear had shortened her patience to the breaking point. Her heart ached from just looking at him, knowing what they could have had, knowing what they'd lost.

Saying nothing, Jared took a sip of his coffee, watching her over the rim of his cup, before pulling out a chair opposite her.

"It's over, Nat," he said softly, laying his hand over hers. Her eyes slid shut for a moment as she savored his touch. It seemed like it had been an eternity since he'd touched her.

Then her eyes open and she blinked to clear her mind. "W-what do you mean?" she asked, afraid to hope, afraid to dream that this nightmare could really be over.

"I'm sorry, Nat," he said softly, lifting her hand to cradle it in his. "Raymond's...dead."

She gasped, her free hand going to her mouth as tears filled her eyes. "Jared, you didn't?" The thought that he could have done something that would put him in jail, or go against his own moral fiber, terrified her.

"No, Nat. I didn't kill him. The police killed him. I went to Kathryn's, and she told me everything. She's stayed in contact with Raymond over the years—well, at least since she left me. Apparently Raymond knew her father, and consequently, knew her. He was paying her to call once a year to check things out, to make sure that you hadn't found the boys. Up until now, she's had nothing to report. This time, well, it was my fault Raymond discovered you'd found the boys. Do you remember the night we went out to dinner and I told you she'd called?"

Natalie nodded.

"Well, I guess I was so pleased that the boys and I had found someone who made us happy that I couldn't help but brag a bit. I told her about you." He shrugged, sipped his coffee, aware that he was so tired every muscle ached. "I told her your name. She reported it to Raymond, apparently unaware of the truth of the situation—that you were the boys' mother and that Raymond had stolen them." Jared shook his head. "Raymond used her just like he used everyone else. She took Raymond's money, and told him everything I'd said. That's how he knew you'd found the boys." He squeezed her hand. "I'm sorry, Nat, for putting you and the boys in this position."

"No, don't be sorry, Jared. You had no way of knowing. So tell me, what happened after you left Kathryn's?"

"She gave me Raymond's address, or at least the last place she knew he was living. I was sorely tempted to go there myself, to teach the man a lesson about terrorizing women and children, but I knew if I did I might not be able to control myself and I'd do something I'd regret." He dragged a hand through his hair. He was so tired even his scalp hurt. "So I called an old friend of Tommy's from the FBI, told him the whole story. He ran Raymond's name through the computer, found the outstanding warrant for kidnapping the boys, along with all the other charges. When they went to arrest Raymond, he resisted. Raymond pulled a gun and..." Jared shrugged. "He left them no choice. He was confirmed dead on the scene."

Jared reached for her hand again, noticing it was icy and trembling. "I'm sorry, Nat. Truly I am." His voice was so full of sympathy that she shook her head fiercely.

"No, don't, please don't be sorry, Jared." Tears filled her eyes, then spilled over. "I'm the one who's sorry. Sorry that his death brings not sadness, but relief, relief from the fear and terror he's inflicted on me for so many years." Wiping her damp face with her free hand, Natalie shook her head. "I know I should have some sympathy for him, feel something, maybe even guilt. He was the boys' father, after all. But I can't. I simply can't." She closed her eyes again and pressed her hand to her frantically beating heart, trying to let the reality of the situation sink in. She and the boys were finally safe and blissfully free from any more of Raymond's threats. So how could she feel guilty? "The boys will finally, truly be safe now." Her watery gaze shifted to his. "Thank you, Jared." She squeezed his hand. "Thank you for giving me something I never thought I'd have." She managed a smile, lifting his hand and pressing it to her lips, wanting to feel contact with him just one last time. "You've given me a sense of peace and freedom from ear, and I didn't think I'd ever have that." She shook her head. "I've lived with this fear for so long…" Her voice clogged with tears and she stopped, glancing down at their entwined hands, her heart still aching because she knew she'd lost this wonderful man. She and the boys might be safe, but she'd lost Jared. And she had no idea how she'd go on without him. "I…don't know how to thank you."

"Well," he began carefully, "if you really want to thank me, you can start by saying you'll stay at least until we can get all this straightened out." His gaze searched hers and he held his breath, afraid to hope. They had to come to a decision about the boys, and that would take time.

"You want me to stay?" she repeated, her heart leaping with joy. "Here?"

Jared sighed. "At least until we get the situation about the boys settled." He blew out a breath, glanced down at his coffee, then back up at her, the ache in his heart visible in his eyes. "Nat, I was very angry and very hurt that you lied to me and betrayed me. I think I still am—"

"Oh, Jared." Tears spilled down her cheeks, and Nat's heart hurt a bit more. "I never meant to lie to you or deceive you." She squeezed his hand, let the tears fall. "I knew from the moment I met you that you were a very special man, the kind of man I'd long ago stopped believing existed. I knew that I was falling in love with you, and knew that I shouldn't, but I couldn't help myself."

"You were falling in love with me?" he asked in surprise, feeling his heart leap in hope.

She smiled, wiped the tears from her cheeks. "Yes, Jared, almost from the start. You were so kind, so gentle, so giving and loving, how could I not love you?" She shook her head. "But I was torn between protecting the boys and loving you." She shrugged. "I knew I couldn't do both. I couldn't love you and lie to you. It's just not me, Jared." She lifted her gaze to his. "But I fell in love with you anyway, knowing you'd probably never be able to forgive me for deceiving you." The truth hurt far more than she'd ever imagined. Finding this kind of man, this kind of love, and then losing it was far more painful than if she had never found it at all.

He studied her beautiful face. "Natalie, I understand why you had to lie and deceive me." He dragged a hand through his hair. "And I'd like to think I would have done the same thing to protect the boys. But I wish you would have trusted me enough to just tell me the whole truth." He rubbed his stubbled jaw with his free hand, unwilling to let go of hers. "I know you did what you did because you love the boys and wanted to protect them. I understand that, because I love them, too, Nat. I always have."

"Oh, Jared." Tears started again, but this time they were tears of hope. "I know that. I've always known that." She had to swallow. "But Jared, you have to understand, I've never had anyone I could trust, at least not since my father died. Especially a man," she added softly. "I was terrified. Trusting you meant placing my life and the boys' lives in your hands."

"I know that, Nat. But that's what you do when you love someone. You trust them. It goes with the territory."

"Jared?" She searched his face. "Before all this happened you asked me to think about making our relationship more personal." She had to take a deep breath before continuing. "Do you think you'll ever be able to trust me again? I mean, really trust me, in order to do that—to make our relationship...personal?"

His smile was slow in coming, but beautiful. "I don't have any choice but to trust you, Nat. You see, I love you, too." He shrugged. "And like I said, if you love someone, you trust them. I understand that now, perhaps better than

ever have before. Trusting is an integral part of love. I
know that what you did you did out of love, out of a need
to protect the boys. I can't say that I would have handled
it any differently."

"Jared?" She was afraid to hope, afraid to believe he
truly meant it. "Do...do you really...love me?"

Cocking his head, he smiled that beautiful smile that always caused her thoughts to scatter like leaves in a fall
wind. "Absolutely, Nat. Without a doubt. I've never been
more sure of anything in my life."

"Oh, Jared." She simply couldn't speak, her heart was
so full. Finally, she blew out a breath, gathered her thoughts
and continued. "I'm sorry I hurt you, and I do trust you,
something I never thought I'd be able to do with another
man. But I do." She held on to his hand for dear life,
wanting his warmth, his nearness like she'd never wanted
anything else.

"I know, hon." Jared lifted his other hand to stroke her
cheek, loving her. "I trust you as well, and I never thought
I'd be able to say that about a woman again, either." He
finally smiled. "Nat, I'd like you to marry me, to stay here
and make a home with me and the boys." He hesitated,
not certain about this part, since they'd never talked about
it. "I'd...I'd like you to have a family with me."

"You want more children?" she asked in surprise. He
was offering her every dream she'd ever had, but never
expected to come true. She wasn't certain her heart could
be any fuller.

He laughed. "Dozens. And a dozen more after that." He
lifted her hand to his lips, closed his eyes, then kissed her.
"Marry me, Nat. Please? Forgive me for behaving like a
jackass, forgive me for not understanding, and most importantly, forgive me for not being there to protect you and

the boys. You're my life, all three of you, and I love you more than life itself. Marry me?''

She leaped from the chair and into his lap, nearly toppling them both over backward. ''Yes!'' She grabbed his face in her hands, planting kisses all over it. ''Yes! Yes! Yes!''

Laughing, Jared wrapped his arms around her and pulled her close, covering her mouth in a kiss that sealed and confirmed their love.

''Jared?'' she murmured against his lips. He groaned, pulling her closer, aching with need.

''Mmm…what?''

''Do you suppose we could get to work on the first dozen pretty soon?''

Jared laughed, hugging her tight. ''You've got a deal, Nat.'' He kissed her again, his heart full. ''A definite deal.''

# Epilogue

*Three months later*

"**D**ad, what's an anniversity?" Terry struggled with the tails of his dress shirt, trying without much success to tuck them into his pants. He wished he could have worn his favorite T-shirt, but his mom had said this was a special anniversity party and he had to dress up.

"Anniversary, Son," Jared corrected, stepping into the twins' bedroom to help them dress. "It's like a birthday, except it's a party to celebrate a special occasion. In this case, we're celebrating when your mom and I got married three months ago." It was hard to believe, Jared thought with a smile. It had been the most wonderful months of his life. He glanced at the boys, then smiled. The most wonderful months of all their lives.

"So do you get presents and stuff?" Timmy asked, frowning as he tried to button his own shirt. He missed a button, making the shirttails uneven. One side wouldn't fit into his pants.

Jared laughed. "Yeah, I guess so." Gently, he hauled Timmy to him and quickly rebuttoned his shirt, helping him tuck it into his pants. With a quick kiss to his son's cheek, he stood, going to the dresser to get a comb.

"Ah jeez, do we gotta comb our hair, too?" Terry complained with a scowl, bouncing on his bed. "I hate combing my hair."

"Yeah, I know, Son," Jared said, trying not to smile, "but it will make your mom happy."

"All right," Terry said, willing to do anything to make his mom happy. She was so cool. It was fun having a mom again. A real mom this time.

"Dad?" Timmy sat on the bed next to his brother. "Is Uncle Jake and Uncle Josh coming for the anniversity party?"

"Yep, even Aunt Rebecca." Jared pulled Timmy into place so he could comb his hair.

"Ah, she's a girl," Terry complained. "She's no fun."

"You know," Jared said carefully, his chest full of pride, "when Mom has our baby, it could be a girl."

"Nah, never," Terry said. "We don't want any smelly girls in the house, do we, Timmy?"

"Nah, no girls, Dad." Timmy glanced up at his father.

Terry scrubbed at his itchy nose, then ran a hand through his hair, mussing it again. "Can't you talk to Mom and ask her for a boy baby?"

"Well…" Jared said, trying not to laugh. "I'll ask her, but I'm not sure Mom has any say in it."

"Ask me what?" Natalie asked with a smile, pushing the boys' door open and stepping into the room. Quickly, er gaze lovingly went over her sons and then shifted to her husband. Her heart filled with love and joy.

"Mom, Timmy and I don't want a girl baby. We want a boy baby, okay?"

Natalie laid a hand to her stomach, which seemed to be growing bigger with each passing day. Just as it had with the boys.

"And how much longer till we get the baby?" Timmy asked, scratching his own nose. "It's been forever."

Natalie laughed, then bent and sat down on the bed next to Terry. Timmy escaped his father's comb and climbed up next to her on the other side, snuggling close.

She glanced up at Jared, saw his smile and smiled in return. "Well, it's going to be about six more months, probably."

"Ah jeez, what's taking so long? I wanted to take the baby to school for show and tell," Terry complained. "I promised all the guys I'd bring my new brother."

"So you want another brother," Natalie said, wrapping an arm around each of her sons and drawing them close.

"Yep," Terry said.

"And what about you?" Natalie asked, turning to Timmy with a smile.

"I...I'd like another brother, too."

She glanced up at her husband, her heart filled with love. "And what about you, Daddy? What do you want?"

Jared grinned at her. "A healthy baby, Nat. Our baby. That's all that's important."

"Well..." she began slowly. "I was going to tell you this later, after dinner—"

"Tell me what?" Instantly worried, Jared moved closer to her, going down on one knee on the floor so they were at eye level. "Are you okay, Nat? You went to the doctor this morning, and with the dinner tonight and all, we haven't really had a chance to talk.'' He glanced at the boys. *Privately,* he added silently.

She laughed at the worry on his face, worry fueled by love, the kind of love she'd never thought she'd ever have. Her heart swelled just a bit more.

"I'm fine, honey,'' she said, reaching for his hand. "Just fine.'' She turned to her sons. "Well, boys, you'll be happy to know that the baby is a boy—''

Whoops of joy filled the air as the twins bounced and high-fived each other across her growing lap.

"Easy, easy, guys.'' Worried they might hurt Nat, Jared took each twin by his hand, setting them on their feet next to him. But he couldn't contain a grin of pure masculine pride as his gaze met his wife's. "So it *is* a boy?''

"Yep,'' she said with a laugh, knowing that in spite of Jared's claim that he didn't care about the sex of the baby, he, too, had wanted a boy. He wanted his own Ryan clan, just like his grandfather Tommy had. "But there's not going to be just one baby boy, hon.''

Confused, he searched her face with his eyes. "What do you mean?''

Natalie sighed, placing a hand on her belly, where the babies were rambunctiously vying for space. "Apparently, according to the doctor, we're going to have *two* baby boys.''

Jared merely stared at her for a moment. "Twins? We're going to have twins?''

She nodded slowly. "Yep.'' She rubbed a hand over her belly again. "Twin boys, from what the doctor tells me.''

"You mean we're getting two brothers instead of just one?'' Terry asked, wriggling in front of his father to see his mom.

"That's right, honey."

"And no smelly girl sisters?"

"Nope, honey, not this time, I'm afraid."

Terry grinned. "Cool."

"Yeah, cool," Timmy added.

"Do…do you mind, honey?" Natalie asked, her gaze going to Jared's.

"Mind?" Jared grabbed her and lifted her into the air, twirling her in a circle before remembering her condition. Gently, he set her down on her feet, keeping his arms around her. "Twins. Nat, there isn't anything—not anything—that could make me happier." His gaze softened as he drew her closer. "I love you, honey." He laid his forehead against hers. "I love you so much."

"Oh, Jared." She lifted her arms and circled them around his neck. "And I love you, too. I've never been happier in my life."

Terry rolled his eyes. "Yuck, they're gonna start kissing again." He turned to his brother. "They're always kissing," he complained. "Let's go find Grandpop and tell him we're each getting a brother."

Jared and Natalie watched the twins race out of the room. "Our children," Jared said with a smile.

"Our boys," Natalie added, nestling closer to her husband and laying his hand on her belly. "Four of them," she added, glancing up at him. "Jared, I'd like to name one of the babies Jesse." Her gaze searched his, not sure how he'd react.

His throat swelled with tears, with love. "Oh, Nat, nothing would please me more."

"I…I know it can never make up for the brother you lost, but—"

He squeezed her hand. "I love the idea, hon." He lifted her hand for a kiss. "Thank you. I love you, Nat."

"I love you, too, honey."

"Let's go celebrate our anniversary, and our family." Taking her hand, Jared led her out of the boys' bedroom, his heart soaring, knowing that no matter what, they were and always would be…a family.

\*     \*     \*     \*     \*

*Don't miss the continuing saga*
*of the Ryan family next month in*

*A FAMILY TO BE,*

*the next installment, Josh's story,*
*in Sharon De Vita's*

SADDLE FALLS

*series.*
*It's on sale in Silhouette Romance*
*in April 2002.*

Award-winning author
# SHARON DE VITA
brings her special brand of romance to

**Silhouette**

## SPECIAL EDITION™
and

### SILHOUETTE *Romance*™

in her new cross-line miniseries

## SADDLE

This small Western town was rocked by scandal when the youngest son of the prominent Ryan family was kidnapped. Watch as new clues about the mysterious disappearance are unveiled—and meet the sexy Ryan brothers...and the women destined to lasso their hearts.

## FALLS

### Don't miss:

**WITH A FAMILY IN MIND**
Silhouette Special Edition, February 2002 #1450

**ANYTHING FOR HER FAMILY**
Silhouette Romance, March 2002 #1580

**A FAMILY TO BE**
Silhouette Romance, April 2002 #1586

**A FAMILY TO COME HOME TO**
Silhouette Special Edition, May 2002 #1468

*Available at your favorite retail outlet.*

**Silhouette®**

*Where love comes alive*™

Silhouette Romance introduces tales of
enchanted love and things beyond explanation
in the new series

# Soulmates

Couples destined for each other are brought
together by the powerful magic of love....

A precious gift brings
## A HUSBAND IN HER EYES
by Karen Rose Smith (on sale March 2002)

Dreams come true in
## CASSIE'S COWBOY
by Diane Pershing (on sale April 2002)

A legacy of love arrives
## BECAUSE OF THE RING
by Stella Bagwell (on sale May 2002)

*Available at
your favorite retail outlet.*

*Where love comes alive*™

Every day is

# A Mother's Day

**in this heartwarming anthology celebrating motherhood and romance!**

**Featuring the classic story "Nobody's Child" by Emilie Richards**
He had come to a child's rescue, and now Officer Farrell Riley was
suddenly sharing parenthood with beautiful Gemma Hancock.
But would their ready-made family last forever?

**Plus two brand-new romances:**

**"Baby on the Way" by Marie Ferrarella**
Single and pregnant, Madeline Reed found the perfect husband in the
handsome cop who helped bring her infant son into the world. But did his
dutiful role in the surprise delivery make J.T. Walker a daddy?

**"A Daddy for Her Daughters" by Elizabeth Bevarly**
When confronted with spirited Naomi Carmichael and her brood of girls,
bachelor Sloan Sullivan realized he had a lot to learn about women!
Especially if he hoped to win this sexy single mom's heart…

*Available this April from Silhouette Books!*

*Silhouette®*
*Where love comes alive™*

Visit Silhouette at www.eHarlequin.com

PSAMD

If you enjoyed what you just read,
then we've got an offer you can't resist!

# Take 2 bestselling love stories FREE!

# Plus get a FREE surprise gift!

---

**Clip this page and mail it to Silhouette Reader Service™**

| **IN U.S.A.** | **IN CANADA** |
|---|---|
| 3010 Walden Ave. | P.O. Box 609 |
| P.O. Box 1867 | Fort Erie, Ontario |
| Buffalo, N.Y. 14240-1867 | L2A 5X3 |

**YES!** Please send me 2 free Silhouette Romance® novels and my free surprise gift. After receiving them, if I don't wish to receive anymore, I can return the shipping statement marked cancel. If I don't cancel, I will receive 6 brand-new novels every month, before they're available in stores! In the U.S.A., bill me at the bargain price of $3.15 plus 25¢ shipping and handling per book and applicable sales tax, if any*. In Canada, bill me at the bargain price of $3.50 plus 25¢ shipping and handling per book and applicable taxes**. That's the complete price and a savings of at least 10% off the cover prices—what a great deal! I understand that accepting the 2 free books and gift places me under no obligation ever to buy any books. I can always return a shipment and cancel at any time. Even if I never buy another book from Silhouette, the 2 free books and gift are mine to keep forever.

215 SEN DFNQ
315 SEN DFNR

| Name | (PLEASE PRINT) | |
|---|---|---|
| Address | Apt.# | |
| City | State/Prov. | Zip/Postal Code |

\* Terms and prices subject to change without notice. Sales tax applicable in N.Y.
\*\* Canadian residents will be charged applicable provincial taxes and GST.
  All orders subject to approval. Offer limited to one per household and not valid to current Silhouette Romance® subscribers.
® are registered trademarks of Harlequin Enterprises Limited.

King Philippe has died, leaving no male heirs to ascend the throne. Until his mother announces that a son *may* exist, embarking everyone on a desperate search for... the missing heir.

Their quest begins March 2002 and continues through June 2002.

On sale March 2002, the emotional
**OF ROYAL BLOOD**
by Carolyn Zane (SR #1576)

On sale April 2002, the intense
**IN PURSUIT OF A PRINCESS**
by Donna Clayton (SR #1582)

On sale May 2002, the heartwarming
**A PRINCESS IN WAITING**
by Carol Grace (SR #1588)

On sale June 2002, the exhilarating
**A PRINCE AT LAST!**
by Cathie Linz (SR #1594)

*Available at your favorite retail outlet.*

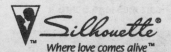

Silhouette®
*Where love comes alive*™

Visit Silhouette at www.eHarlequin.com
SRRW4